Lunchtime Chronicles:

Mystery Meat

By Keta Kendric

Messy Mandy Presents:
The Lunchtime Chronicles Season 3
Mystery Meat

Cover art by Wicked Smart Designs
Editors: One More Glance, A.L. Barron

ISBN: 978-1-7332914-5-3/ Mystery Meat

Table of Contents

Dedication

To all of the twisted, wicked, and chaos loving readers who gave me and my writing a chance and continue to read my work: I am grateful for you. Your support means everything. Thank You.

To the amazing authors of the Lunchtime Chronicles Season 3: Siera London, L. Loren, Posey Parks, and Sonja B. The amount of knowledge sharing, encouragement, time, and teamwork that was poured into this project blew me away and made me proud to be a part of the group. Thank you for this extraordinary experience. In my southern accent, *We family now!*

Welcome to Messy Mandy Presents:

The Lunchtime Chronicles Season 3

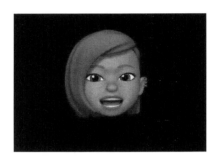

The Lunchtime Chronicles was launched by Author Siera London at the Interracial Author's Expo in Daytona Beach in 2019 with the novella, Whipped. The erotic romance novellas are presented like a magazine issue, lunchtime themed, and released by a diverse group of authors each season. For the latest gossip and updates from your favorite Lunchtime Chronicles authors, please follow the Facebook page: Lunchtime Dish with Messy Mandy.

Mystery Meat Synopsis:

Camina: Receiving a mysterious black card from a stranger to a place called 'The Market' should have been my first clue. How was I supposed to know that this market was as non-traditional as the items they put on display?

Colson: It was her voice that drew my attention, and eavesdropping on her personal conversation had dragged me deeper into her life. Since I had invited myself into her world, it was only fair that I extended her an invitation into mine.

Warning: This novella is an interracial romance that contains strong language, explicit sexual content, BDSM, and is intended for adults. If you have no problems with any of the aforementioned, please continue, and discover the *Wicked Truth*.

CHAPTER ONE

Camina

After twelve hours of turning wrenches and rebuilding a car's engine, I ignored my body's demand for sleep and forced it to perform one last task. The evening traffic on Houston's Loop 610 had no mercy during my race home for a quick shower and clothing change.

As the owner and head mechanic in my auto shop, I worked insane but rewarding hours. I had served six proud years in the military with a MOS (military occupational specialty) of wheeled-vehicle mechanic. Once I completed my service, I invested my savings in my shop and worked my ass off to make it a success.

Meeting my cousin, Kenzie, for a last-minute dinner invitation was not how I had planned to spend my midweek evening. However, I was determined to make a valid effort to establish a social life outside of work.

When I arrived at the restaurant and was escorted to our table, my mood took a nosedive when the dinner invitation was for a party of four. My cousin had ambushed me again, shoving another blind date down my throat. Her new husband, David, sat next to her with a grin on his face, aware of the set up.

Mindful not to complain, I reminded myself that Kenzie was looking out for me. My blind date, however, was another story. The 1970s wanted Marvin back. He was thirty-six, a few years older than me, but he dressed like he was fifty.

Case in point; the thigh-clenching, shit-brown bell-bottoms he wore that I knew were hiding platform shoes. To top off the throwback look was the low cut, big collared, long sleeve striped and yellow silk shirt.

When had I become the person that was reduced to taking date handouts? My loser status had sunk so low that I was preparing to take my seat in *rock bottom,* a place lower than hell.

***

Fast-forward two hours, and I was back at my house, angry at myself for the decisions I had made tonight. *"How could I have been so fucking stupid to bring this man back to my house?"* Was I desperate? Had I allowed a despairing level of self-pity to flow into my system? A glutton for punishment, this had turned out to be one of *the most* disappointing hump-days of my life.

My date's voice, my current view of him, and even his erratic movements began to fade into the background as I zoned out and concentrated on my weekend plans. I needed to decide what I wanted to prepare for my family's potluck gathering. Although busy trudging through our hectic lives, we managed to do a good job of coming together once or twice a month to break bread together.

Maybe I could make a few desserts for the upcoming event, and I also needed to check my supplies and pull together my weekly grocery list. I allowed my thoughts to rage on because they were more entertaining than the efforts my *date* was making to keep my attention.

A series of rough jerks were what prompted me to break out of my mind and pay attention to the current reality of my uneventful hump-day. The hard pumps that Marlin was delivering to my body had disturbed my thoughts and added weight to the all-time low I had reached. Or was his name Morgan? Anyway, he was on top of me, had been for a while now, *rutting* as he called it, shoving into me with hard grunts that left every vein in his sweat-slicked body protruding.

You *knew* my sex life was shit when sex with my B.O.B, battery-operated boyfriend, was better than with the last three men who had crawled between my legs and called themselves rocking my world. The truth of the matter was that my world hadn't even been tilted.

"Tell me how good it feels, baby," Marcus demanded.

Good enough for me to be thinking about a grocery list.

"So, so, good," I forced out, lying my ass off so he would hurry the fuck up and get off me. I'd promised myself that I would be more accommodating when dealing with dates because I'd shoved the last two men off in the middle of the act and told them in not so nice words, *"Get your lazy dick-stroking, don't know how to fuck if I gave you a class, ass off of me."*

I had followed up my commentary by shoving them out of the door while they cursed me out and attempted to get dressed. I'd even tried to shove one man out of his own house before realizing that I was the one that needed to be leaving. So, here I was, letting that fourth glass of wine I'd consumed do its job.

"You like this dick, don't you?" he asked, huffing and puffing like what he was doing was setting my world on fire when he hadn't even ignited a spark. His question had broken into my chain of thoughts, right when I was deciding on pound cake or sock-it-to-me cake for my upcoming family event.

Shut the fuck up before I call AAA, you broken-down-dick-bastard, was my real response.

"Um hum," I groaned instead, biting into the curse words sitting at the tip of my tongue.

What happened to the days when men took command of their dicks and sent it into the pussy like a soldier who wasn't coming out until he sought and destroyed every hot spot? It was a fucking shame what sex amounted to for me now. The shit was depressing.

Lord help him, I mumbled to myself, shaking my head in growing frustration. He was thrusting at my pussy with such aggression, you'd think I had snatched his girlfriend's engagement ring and announced that I was bringing it to his wife. I didn't mind it fast and hard, but the least he could do was make sure I was enjoying the sex too.

"Your dick is so big and long—" Fuck, I couldn't remember his name. "It's touching the back." The lie paid off because he started to roar into my ear, his hot breath blowing like a blow dryer set on high.

Thank you, Jesus! I rolled my eyes as the fuck-deficient asshole was nearing the end of his useless pounding. He had missed every erogenous zone, chilled my hot spots into ice cubes, and made my arousal hormones nauseous.

Never again. The son of a bitch was getting his happy ending, and I was lying there talking myself out of beating him about the head with one of my dildos.

"Girl, you got some good pussy," he yelled out, trembling on top of me while I swiped a drop of his sweat from my cheek. He wasn't even going to check to see if I was going to come.

This was what I got for taking my cousin's advice about broadening my horizons and going out on blind dates and shit. Now, I was lying here with a messy pussy that was beaten all to hell for no reason, and my poor kitty was still hungry. Next time I saw Kenzie, I was cursing her the fuck out.

The way this man had teased me at dinner about what he could do in bed had tempted me, talking about his nickname was the Candy Licker. If expanding my horizons led me to this kind of fucked up *fuck*, I was taking my chances on my own.

CHAPTER TWO

Camina

Months later.

The eye-closing inhale I breathed did nothing to call forth the positive vibes I needed to apply to my current reality. Still, the sight of my honey-butter biscuit flying across the table and bopping my cousin upside her head gave me a spark of satisfaction.

Leaning across the table, I bit into my syllables, spitting the sound through clenched teeth to protect the ears of the other diners from the arsenal of curse words I was prepared to launch.

"Will you please announce louder to the rest of this fucking restaurant that I have been on a six-month dry spell? Why don't you tell them that my fucking pussy is so unused it probably needs an EEG test to check for activity down there before I put it back on the market?"

My cousin laughed her ass off at my depressing ass sex life like it was a joke. I rolled my eyes at her, cackling so hard her shoulders quaked.

"Camina," she called, dragging out my name. "You have to keep trying. Between me and the N2U dating app you've been using, it's only a matter of time before you find someone. You just need to relax and be more open." She leaned in closer, lowering her voice. "By open, I do mean opening your legs more and giving up some pussy."

My back stiffened at my cousin's crass words, hoping her so-called advice hadn't traveled past our booth. If so, she was going to make this a lunchtime to remember for some unsuspecting patrons.

"You're too hard on men. They want a soft lady, not the hardcore ex-soldier or ball-crushing mechanic you are at work. If you learned how to be a little more submissive, I promise you; you would have a good man in no time."

I hissed at her while glancing around the restaurant, thankful that no one was paying us any attention.

"One of David's friends is dying to go out with you," Kenzie added with a sneaky smirk plastered on her face.

Kenzie and David had met and married after a two-month courtship. I wasn't knocking my cousin's methods as she and David appeared to be happy, but what worked for her was not working for me.

I stared at her moving her advice-giving lips, letting her words flow in one ear while dumping them out the other.

"Why don't you let me handle my love-life? I *have* had successful relationships before," I stated, cutting into one of her sentences.

"By successful, you mean, going up to a cheating ex and punching his lights out in a crowded five-star restaurant? The shit was trending on social media and made it onto the Lunchtime Dish with Messy Mandy."

Thankfully, my face had been blurry on the recording, or the world, namely Houston, would have known who was acting a damned fool in a local restaurant.

"What about the one you hog-tied and left in the trunk of his car when you found out he was married."

Was I really that bad?

I squinted in thought, my gaze locked on Kenzie's.

"How about I bring up your stalking tendencies? Or better yet, let's talk about the one you caught cheating. You slung hot grits on him and the woman he was cheating with and sent them to the hospital with first and second-degree burns."

Kenzie's eyes fell before her head sunk into her shoulders. She didn't want to hear any of her own mess and had the nerve to look embarrassed.

A ping from my phone called my attention, an update from my N2U dating profile. Kenzie had no idea that the second date I had found on the app months ago had invited me to a group outing to meet up with him. When I arrived at the location he'd given me, the group was standing around, socializing. It wasn't until I sat in the circle of chairs they had arranged that I understood the damn man had invited me to his AA meeting. *Who does that?*

I was tempted to report him to Deja Cummings, the creator of N2U, but she was friends with Amanda 'Messy Mandy' Murphy. The last thing I wanted was to become the trending topic on, The Lunchtime Dish, with Mandy spilling the tea about the food fight I'd started at an AA meeting because my blind date hadn't turned out the way I'd expected.

Kenzie aimed a stiff finger in my direction, dragging me from one of my dating nightmares.

"Some men like aggressive women, but you have to figure out how to tone it down."

A deep frown settled on my forehead. "That's what I'm doing," I hissed at her. "Didn't I let the last one walk away with his ego intact?"

She could purse her lips all she wanted to—she knew damn well that 1970s throwback she'd set me up with wasn't going to cut it.

"I'm not always aggressive, especially if I find a man who knows what he's doing," I defended. "It's hard to tone down my aggression when a man comes at me like *the man* and shows me I have more bark in my middle finger than he has in his whole body. Give me a man who knows what the fuck he's doing, and I'll sit my ass down and let him do his thing."

I needed to change the subject because talking about dating was channeling my anger.

"Family potluck is coming up. I decided that I'm going to do the meats. Maybe some ribs, a roast, or steak. What are you making?"

She shrugged, her turned-up lip and unfocused gaze was highlighting her disinterest in where I was leading the conversation. "If cousin Janice brings them six badass kids of hers, I'll get those cheap-ass ready-made pies from the supermarket."

She stared under her lashes before her face transformed and revealed a conniving smile. "Like I was saying about David's friend, Kyle. He saw you at our wedding, and David forgot to mention it to you. A few days ago, he asked about you again," she stated, switching the subject back.

"Not that shit again. No," I whisper-yelled while shaking my head vigorously. "I'm capable of finding my own dates."

Pity covered her face once she zoomed in on the sadness I attempted to cover with a tight smile.

"Damn shame." She shook her head. "You got a nice fit body and can be pretty if you relax your face for more than a few seconds at a time. I vote that you open up them legs until the right man lands between them."

"Lord knows my ass is lonely."

Kenzie's ears perked. Had I spoken that shit out loud? I kept talking in an effort to block the set-my-pussy-loose-on-the-world sermon she was set to preach. Truth was, I missed being held and feeling the smooth, hard warmth of a man's body next to mine.

Some people assumed I was a lesbian because I wore coveralls and fixed cars for a living, but in the last few years, I just couldn't find anyone to satisfy my needs. However, my personal preference where sex was concerned had never changed—I loved dick.

Dating any of my employees was out of the question. The riff-raff who stumbled into the garage were old enough to be my grand-pappy, and the rest looked like the living manifestations of Hep-C, Chlamydia, and Syphilis.

The frown on Kenzie's face had grown intense enough to reach into my thoughts. I was clueless about what I'd missed, but the hand she had caressing her belly,

coupled with the chair version of the pee-pee dance relieved me of having to search for a response.

"Excuse me. This baby is barely the size of a lemon,
and it feels like he's playing ping pong with my bladder,"
Kenzie blurted.

She dashed away from the table before I could comment. She had met, married, and gotten pregnant within a
four-month time span. She was thirty-two, and I was
thirty-four, but the way she was moving, you'd think our
eggs were giving us the evil-eye while holding up a stop-
watch.

Now that I was alone, I honed in on the conversations taking place around me, specifically, the guy at my
back. He sat on the other side of the glass of our booth,
speaking to his waitress, thanking her for her service before handing her back his bill.

He was moving behind me now, preparing to leave,
and I prayed the poor man hadn't heard any of my and
Kenzie's conversation. I dropped my gaze to my phone,
pretending to be interested in my social media feeds now
that I was aware of him.

His steps sounded before I got a glimpse of the long
lines of his legs covered in navy slacks from the corner of
my eye. His abrupt stop froze me, and before I could
glance up, his hand jetted out in front of me. I yanked myself away from him with my fist clenched tight, but he
walked away as swiftly as he'd stopped, leaving a business card on the table in front of me.

My head snapped up, and caught a glimpse of his
retreating back. His dwindling features had a tight hold of

my attention, making me edge up higher in my seat, but he was already turning into the wait area and out of view.

Based on his hand and the small portion of skin I'd seen, he was Caucasian. He had short dark hair, and a stylish dark suit was draped nicely over his tall, medium build.

I glanced down at the shiny black business card he'd left with the fancy gold font. 'The Market,' I read. He must have heard the part of our conversation about my upcoming family gathering. I was hosting it at my house the following weekend, so checking out a new market wasn't a bad idea.

While studying the card, I noticed that there was only the title, address, and the caption that bolstered the best selection of meats in the city. The back of the card was blank. Not even a number was listed. The man's strategy was a good one, as no website or number meant you'd have to show up in person to check out what they offered.

An automatic smile surfaced as past family get-togethers popped into my head. There was never a dull moment because drama would always start up and secrets were spilled every time.

My mother, Claudette Harrison, didn't hesitate to toss out subtle hints of her exploits with younger men. It had taken her a decade to start dating again after my father, Clifton, had died of liver cancer unexpectantly. He was the love of her life, and since she'd vowed never to give her heart to another, she was a low-key cougar who released a growl every once in a while.

My younger brother Caleb did nothing but keep scorecards on the different men he'd bedded. My cousin

Kenzie and I were the closest, so she rode me the hardest about my nonexistent love life.

And I couldn't forget about my aunt and uncle with their old-time ways. Uncle Ralph was my mother's only and older brother, and he and his wife Lou-ann didn't hesitate to drop old-school knowledge about dating and life in general on us *young-ins* as they called us. According to them, we were doing it all wrong, and they were very outspoken with their advice.

It had been a while since I'd hosted at my house and a touch of excitement hit me at the prospect of seeing everyone together again. I pinched the black card between my fingers, plucking it with my middle one before I shoved it into the side of my purse just as Kenzie was returning.

"You ready?" she questioned while retaking her seat.

I nodded.

Once the check was paid, and we stepped outside the restaurant, we drew each other into a tight hug before she climbed into her Uber just as mine was driving up. I would sometimes forgo driving into the city to avoid the hectic Houston traffic and the hazards of parking.

I gave one last wave to my cousin before I ducked into the back of the white Nissan Versa waiting for me.

***

Colson

The vibrant activities of the night shrouded city below competed with its twinkling lights for my attention.

Absently, I swirled the amber liquid in my glass while untangling warring thoughts of dating in my brain.

The woman whose conversation I'd eavesdropped on in the restaurant during lunch wouldn't stay off my mind. Sitting and listening to her defend her dating life made me laugh. It had also led me to sympathize with the parts of her life that mimicked experiences similar to mine.

She was facing the issue of being caught up in the rut of wanting something but at the same time being unable to find the right person to share herself with in order to get what she needed. The back and forth and failed attempts at finding her match probably made her question if she was the problem.

I hadn't left a woman a card in months, but when I'd sat observing her dark reflection in the booth's glass surface, it didn't take much for me to become immersed in her world. Now, after giving her the card, fear tugged like a noose tied around my heart, telling me I had made a mistake. I had to find a way to be at 'The Market' when and if she showed up. Otherwise, I'd drive myself crazy wondering if she and I could give each other what we needed.

Shit!

Why hadn't I just broken my own rules about dating and asked her out instead?

CHAPTER THREE

Camina

A week later.

After informing my family that I had a long week-end off and would be providing the meats for our upcoming family gathering, I decided to pay 'The Market' a visit. I'd taken this Friday off since Monday was Memorial Day, creating myself a four-day weekend. It also gave me a much-needed break because lying under a car even in an air-conditioned garage in May was exhausting work.

After coffee, a bagel, and a quick shower, I hopped into a pair of jeans, sandals, and a fitted T-shirt before ordering an Uber. The black card for 'The Market' held a bit of intrigue and had me interested to see what they had to offer.

It took forty minutes to travel twenty miles into the heart of the city. My eyes skimmed the skyscrapers that loomed above the street like big, intimidating bullies. A mix of swirling people and cars poured energy into the atmosphere that gave the city its strong pulse. The place was brimming with enough power to lure you into the fray of its movements and temp you to stay.

We were downtown, nestled among five-star hotels and over-priced office spaces. I shot the driver a quick, "Thank you," before exiting the car and paying my fare with a few finger swipes over the face of my phone.

I approached the building with a curious frown, ignoring the impolite people bumping into me. How were they running a market out of *this* building with its high-end boutiques and restaurants?

Though reluctant, my curiosity kept me moving until I stepped through the shiny gold-trimmed doors that automatically parted for me. The lobby was a bustling landscape of elegantly designed furnishings and massive wall paintings that complimented shiny, silver accents and an extravagant crystal chandelier that hung in the ceiling like the crown jewel of the building. People milled about, some pushing luggage as they checked in, and others were being escorted out to waiting cars.

This was the luxurious Keynote Hotel known to house many celebrities as well as the infamous Pixie Dust restaurant which was always booked-up and bragged about by the most esteemed food critics.

Confusion polluted my brain, leaving me scratching my head and flipping the black card over my fingers. My dragging approach to the reception desk drew the attention of two of the six front-desk attendants.

"Checking in?" One of those young male attendants whose name-tag read, Vance, asked as I casually strolled to the counter.

"No." I flashed him the card. "Looking for 'The Market.' Have you been there before?" His face didn't give away anything as he presented his practiced smile.

"'The Market' is *very* exclusive. You have to be invited to even walk through the door. I've worked here for two years and have only ever walked past it."

His update added weight to my heavy curiosity about the place. Were they selling the Rolls-Royce of meats in there?

"It's on the second level." Vance pointed at the stairs. "You can take the elevator, but it's faster if you take the stairs."

"Okay. Thank you." I flashed him a smile since his had never lost its customer service luster.

The further I burrowed into this scene, the more I got that prickly sense that something wasn't right.

Once I cleared the stairs and the short expanse of the hall that followed, I walked up to the tall doors and stood in place, taking in my reflection in the mirrored tint. There was no missing the golden letters on the hallway wall that spelled out 'The Market.'

I swallowed my reluctance and shoved at the tall glass entrance doors, but nothing happened. A quick inspection showed a single red blinking dot that sat above a card slot. I glanced down at the card in my hand before I shoved it into the slot, and watched as the light turned green. The doors parted, releasing a refreshing scent carried by a cool breeze that teased the edges of my hair.

The attendant downstairs was right—you weren't getting into this place without an invite. *Why had I been invited?*

The first few steps I took past the entrance, I was greeted by a set of commercial-ready white teeth sitting in the handsome face of a man who appeared to be in his late-twenties. Dark hair, tall, fit, and polished in a gray designer suit, he was standing behind a reception area, waiting with a barely-contained smile.

"Welcome to 'The Market.' We are so happy you decided to visit us today." He didn't offer his name, so neither did I.

"Thank you," I mouthed, but my attention was being cast throughout the space. The gold-plated letters on the dark gray of the marble wall behind the reception area stood out elegantly and made it appear that I'd stepped into a high-end spa rather than a market.

The place looked expensive and carried a regal air. The wall of windows to my right was tinted dark and showed off an eye-catching view of the city. The tint allowed the room to maintain a romantic ambiance.

Gleaming surfaces, recessed art displays on the walls, and strategically-placed floral arrangements served their visual and aromatic purposes. The fragrance was light and refreshing, a mood-enhancing scent like lavender kissing warm earth with a hint of mint.

Instrumental music crooned softly from an unseen source, turned down low enough that your ears chased the sound. Now that I had thoroughly scoped out the reception area, I was picking up serious spa vibes. I stepped up to the counter and rested my forearms against the cool marble while continuing to survey my surroundings.

"What is this place?" I asked the man before glancing down at the card in my hand like it held magic. "I was planning a family gathering and assumed I was about to shop for some choice selections of meats. I'm starting to believe I was given this card by mistake."

The man gave the card a casual glance before putting those gray eyes, shining with mischief, back on me.

"Those cards are not given out by mistake." He pointed at the door behind me. "The door wouldn't have opened if you hadn't been invited. A black card means that one of our exclusive members gave it to you directly."

He leaned across the counter with flashes of excitement highlighting his handsome features. "A hundred of those cards are given out a year, which means the giver thought that you were deserving of the services our market offers. Also, once you triggered the door, an alert was sent out so that we could ensure that you have multiple selections available."

Was he insinuating drugs or some other black market shit?

"And what kind of services are you talking about? I work hard to live a trouble-free, *legal* life. If you have something illegal going on here, you can take this card back and give it to someone else."

He waved away the notion and widened that gleaming smile. "I can assure you that everything we do here is legal."

"Is this some sort of high-end spa?" I asked to make sure we were on the same page.

"Yes, of sorts, but we are determined to go above and beyond the treatments you receive at traditional spas. The difference is that we offer a one-time service. Our goal is to provide you with such a pleasurable experience that you will give us a well-deserved recommendation afterward."

A deep crease marred my forehead. He'd piqued my interest. However, a nagging voice kept telling me, *you can't afford this place, and it might not be legal.*

"You only take people by recommendation? No call-ins? No walk-ins?"

"That's correct. We value our exclusivity. Word of mouth recommendations, or a card like the one you're holding is the only acceptable ways into this market."

He stepped from behind the counter and stood in front of a wall of spirits.

"What would you like to drink?" he questioned, motioning his hands to the drool-worthy display behind him. The sparkling dark glass of the shelves that made up the full wall to the left of me was stocked with nothing but top-shelf alcohol. The area was like one big color-changing diamond.

"Water," I replied, although I was thirsting for something stronger. The urge I'd had to turn around and leave the place was dying by the second because my curiosity had roared to life.

"Come closer," he called with a flirty flash in his gaze and a head gesture. He ushered his hand towards the elegant marble-topped bar area, equipped with three black leather-covered bar stools. I hadn't noticed the full set up of the area until I took the necessary steps closer.

"Everything you see here is on the house. Instead of water, might I suggest a glass of Chateau Latour? It's guaranteed to make your palate weep."

A bold and intense choice. Being a mechanic did not exclude me from being knowledgeable about wine. I'd also traveled and explored the world at least twice a year. Early on, when I visited many tastings, I thought of becoming a sommelier because of my wine knowledge but was content being somewhat of a connoisseur.

"Since you put it that way. Please. I'd love a glass."

My gaze was fixed, not only on how much he poured, but how he handled the bottle too. I knew wine enough to know that he'd poured generously from a thousand-dollar bottle. I also eyeballed the hell out of him to make sure he didn't slip me anything.

I was clinging to my trust, not as strongly as when I'd stepped in, but I wasn't willing to let go right away. I accepted the offered glass without hesitation, allowing the wine to breathe before I gave it a whirl. The swirl produced legs that flowed down the glass like a group of graceful dancers, giving me a good hint at the alcohol potency. A calming sniff made the rich scents waft up my nose and my tongue watered for the first sip.

The dark red liquid poured over my tongue, so bold and tasty, it was like a flavor party energizing my taste buds. Blackberry and currant, raspberry, and hints of spices surfaced. This wine had a depth to its personality, and the host was right because my palate wept with delight. He appeared pleased by my reaction, his sparkling smile widening and lighting up his gray eyes.

"You like?"

"Yes. I love," I replied. A subtle warmth was spreading through me at a leisurely pace after just one sip.

"Good. You can relax and enjoy the wine while I check on the selections for you."

A quick roll of my shoulders reminded me that I'd not been massaged in months, sacrificing my *me time* to work overtime. I sat sipping my wine and blatantly watched the sensual movements of my attendants suit over his fit body as he walked away. I didn't understand what type of selection he was going to prepare, but the element of surprise kept me buzzing with intrigue.

The wine settled into my system, plying me with happy vibes that caused a little giggle to bubble up from my chest. What was I about to see? Was it a collection of massage therapists? Exclusive spa packages?

Just when I was polishing off the glass of sparkling optimism, the mirrored doors to the back of the suite sprang open. The doors were probably two-way mirrors as I'd felt eyes on me a few times. The man who had greeted me returned, looking like a tall shot of straight sex appeal. The wine had loosened me up, so I didn't skirt my eyes away as he strolled up and stood next to me. The first thing he reached for was my glass.

"The selections will be on display for you momentarily. We have four available today, and I hope that you find them worth your time. Let me refresh your drink," he offered before I could ask specifics about the selections. A part of me wanted to know the answer as much as I wanted to be surprised.

"No. I can't have another. I don't want to leave here staggering," I stated with a wave of the hand.

"I insist. We want you to have a good time, and we'd never allow you to leave in any condition that may be

harmful to you. As I mentioned earlier, we work from recommendations based on your experience, so keeping you
happy and safe is our number one priority."

Good to know. My smile widened. "In that case, I
wouldn't mind having another."

My ass was about to be tipsy because this wasn't one
of those cheap twenty-dollar bottles that I kept around for
family. I took the glass with a smile, unwilling to let the
good stuff go to waste, especially if it was free.

"When I take you back to the viewing area, you are
encouraged to smell, touch, and taste as much as you like.
We recommend it so that you can get a better sense of
what you may like. We wouldn't want you to finalize a
choice and later end up disappointed because you didn't
test it out."

I nodded and sipped.

"We will allow you as much time as you need to
make your selection. Once you have chosen, we will give
you a questionnaire that we encourage you to be brutally
honest when completing it."

My brows creased. Was he being purposely vague?
Was this how the rich shopped for spa services?

"This way," the man said, ushering me towards the
doors before placing a strong hand on the small of my
back. He shoved the doors open and allowed me to walk
in before him.

A dim view met me, drenching my vision in darkness and leaving me squinting. I narrowly made out the
shiny marble floors and a dark curtain that spanned the
length of the large, high-ceiling room. The upbeat rhythm
pouring from hidden speakers was more up-tempo here

than in the reception area, and the low thumping beats matched the anticipation rolling through me.

Strategically-placed stage lighting gradually brightened and was thankfully aimed at the black curtains billowing before me. A hardy sip of wine teased my taste buds before sliding down my throat with smooth ease, but did nothing to take the edge off my heightened eagerness.

"You guys sure go out of your way to present your selections," I stated. My natural, curious nature had me a few steps from walking up to those curtains and snatching them back myself.

"We are confident that we have the best to offer, so we present them in the best possible light to you."

He lifted a hand, and the curtains began to slide apart. At first, I didn't know what I was looking at. It was a huge fancy wooden display made of black lacquered wood, tall in height, and it contained four presentation sections.

Each square was positioned within its own section with a display stand jetting out below the opening. The section openings were no larger than two by two and certainly not large enough to display a full person. What the heck were they planning to show me?

The host stood a few paces before me at the first exhibit area, positioned so that he faced me and was at the left of the opening.

"Your first choice is a nine-inch selection with a thick circumference to provide a pleasing stretch."

When I paired the host's words with what was being presented, wine was sprayed all over the place, blasting past my lips from the shock that rocked my system. The light complexion of a torso filled the square opening, and a *stiff dick*, hard and plump was what the host was gesturing his hand toward.

This market wasn't a spa in *any* traditional sense of the word. The black card and the invitation-only exclusivity were all about the *meat*, literally.

"Deep beige with a group of prominent veins that run the span of the shaft," the host continued his monologue like I hadn't spit wine into the air like confetti. The bright light allowed me to clearly see *everything* the host described.

Without mentioning my erratic response, he simply removed his handkerchief and handed it to me. I robotically dotted my mouth and chin clean, thankful that the wine had mellowed me enough not to release the high pitched scream that would have otherwise accompanied my outburst.

Despite the currents of excitement still coursing through me, I hadn't shied away from the sight of live dick. I eyeballed it even as I leaned closer and prepared to speak to the host.

"I'll admit, I haven't had the best of luck with men, but I have never paid for dick, and I'm sure it's illegal to do so." I wouldn't have minded some grade-A dick, but I'd be damned if I paid for it.

"And we'd be insulted if you tried to pay," he replied, putting an end to my thoughts of making dick purchases. His words had me glaring between him and the spot-lighted dick that was jutting with power against the display table like it was eager for my attention.

"You received an invite, which means whatever you see, and choose or not choose, is of no cost to you. Your time and the card in your hand is all we will require in exchange for whatever choices you make. You can walk away at any point. It's completely up to you."

The man at the restaurant had heard my conversation with Kenzie and must have felt sorry for me since this was where his card had led.

"Will you stay and view the rest of the choices?" The host asked in a pleading tone with hope filling his handsome face.

If he thought I was leaving, he was sadly mistaken. I had paused long enough to piece together all the clues I had missed. Him reminding me the card got me whatever the hell I wanted had sealed the deal as far as I was concerned. I took a step closer, and the dick jumped at my approach, causing my eyes to widen, and my heart rate to knock a little faster.

The host chuckled. "Based on this selection's level of excitement, I'd say that he likes you."

I leaned closer to the host, shielding my words like the dick had ears. "Can he see me?"

"Yes. Does it excite you to know that you can make him react like this without physical contact?"

Why the fuck was I getting turned on all of a sudden? My cheeks were hot, and my starving pussy was starting to smell food. Another step drew me closer as the bright light put the beautiful piece of meat on full display.

"Touch it," the host urged.

My grip tightened around the long stem of the wine glass like it might around that dick. Instead of reaching out like I wanted to, I took another sip. The dick lifted like it was being manipulated by strings before falling back against the display with a fleshy smack, waving me closer.

It didn't have to tell me twice. I reached out and ran a feathery-light finger, from root to tip. It jumped right before I removed my finger, licking my fingertip. I missed the way a real dick felt. *Velvety. Hot. Hard.*

A silly smirk sat on my lips, and like the sexually starved loser I was, I stood there staring and admiring the meat. The host moved, breaking me from the trance I'd fallen into. He shifted to the next display, but the first one remained in place, thick and enticing, not letting me forget that he was still there.

When the host ushered a hand towards the next selection, a set of flexing abs on tight skin was highlighted against the dark wood surface of the display case. The splendid cut of meat attached to that manly body revealed itself, and my throat went so dry it hurt to swallow.

The host was saying something because his lips were moving, but my ears were closed, and my eyes were wide. I took in everything this time. Perfectly tanned skin was the background for a beautiful dick a few shades darker. A deep peachy-pink, the skin was pulled tight around a jutting mass of the most beautiful piece of live art I'd ever seen.

This one was at least ten inches and had a few veins running up the shaft along the top and sides. The veins resembled lightning bolts like the dick had its own personality. It was so stiff that I saw the pulse beating in the veins, flowing with raging eagerness.

I released the grip I had on the wine glass and found myself reaching out despite what the host was saying. Awed by the sight of it, my head shook in a mix of disbelief and admiration. This one held a magnificent charm that drew me in, its long, thick shaft and tight, bulging head was a hypnotic force that called to my senses. So yep, I commenced to stroking the dick of a man whose face I'd never seen.

The first stroke was surreal like I was hung up in a dick daydream. The flesh was warm and soft with hard strength beneath a slick velvety covering. It flexed, making me jerk my hand back from the feeling of the power it possessed.

"Please. Don't be afraid. Keep stroking it," the host urged. His tone was low and husky like he was getting off on watching me stroke a stranger's dick. "You can taste it if you'd like. It has been medically confirmed that this display consists of the cleanest meat in the city," he encouraged, his tone dropping deeper.

Another sip of wine shot straight to my head and assisted in helping me lose my inhibitions. I reached out and stroked, lightly at first, watching it wave like it was playing at teasing my hand. This meat selection apparently had a direct line to my pussy because hot sparks of energy made her clench with every stroke I delivered.

Was I hearing things, or was that the heavy breathing of whoever this dick belonged to? The anxious movement of the torso behind the black fixture made my brow rise. He was enjoying the way I fondled him.

The lights were aimed downward so that pools of darkness sat at eye-level, leaving the men an area to watch while I assessed their meat. Whoever this was, he wasn't hiding his enjoyment. His body moved sensually against the display, swaying with the slow movement of my hand. My actions, slight as they were, turned him on enough that his reaction had me squeezing my thighs together.

I took the gorgeous dick more firmly, gripping the underside at the base and stroking up the strong length. Damn, I was loving how it was so alive and not anything like the silicone lover I had fucked the ridges off at home. Reluctantly, I let go, remembering that I had two more selections waiting. The host had been mindful to hand me disinfectant wipes after each observation.

My hand glided up and down the shaft of the third selection until the tips of my fingers flirted with the leaking head and triggered a moan, the sound muffled behind the display. This one was also a ten incher.

"We have had a few not continue with the service because they claimed the selections were too large. You don't have a problem with the sizes, do you?"

I cocked an are-you-fucking-kidding-me gaze at the man, and he nodded at my expression with a pleased smile. Even if I did have a problem, it was one I was willing to deal with when the time came.

A smile chased my hard swallow when I accepted that I liked this erotic world I'd been invited into. However, this third selection hadn't been nearly as enticing as number two. I kept glancing back at it as if to say, *"Don't worry, baby, I'll be back."*

The host moved over to the final selection to conduct his presentation. This one was immediately on the *do not engage* section for me. It was so long I mistook it for the man's arm. I wanted a good fucking, not to have my insides eviscerated. Although I got an arousing kick out of interacting with something so beastly, my eyes kept going back to number two, Mr. Ten-inch dream meat.

After the final inspections, my decision was an easy one. I returned to number two, unable to stop myself from pointing out to the host the cut of meat I desired most.

"Excellent choice. Let's go and take care of the questionnaire while your choice prepares for the next segment."

"Next segment?" I questioned, unsure how this all worked. A glance over my shoulder showed the choices were gone, but my gaze landed on the second display panel.

"Yes. The selection gets dressed and ready for the next step in the process," he answered but hadn't really said a damned thing. I believed I was finally starting to get their game plan. Their goal was to keep the element of surprise in play as part of their service. The host certainly had done his job well. From the moment I entered, not once had he revealed anything that would give me a hint of what went on here.

We stepped into a high-end office, off to the right side of the stage area, where he directed me to a plush black leather chair in front of the black and silver desk with powder chrome accents before taking my glass.

"Would you like me to refresh this for you?"

"No. One more glass, and you are going to be finding me a place to sleep."

"We can arrange it if that is what you would like?"

I waved the man off. "What is this all about? Are you telling me a stranger gave me this card—" I lifted the black card and continued. "—to stroll in here and pick out the perfect meat. And I can do whatever I want with this *meat,* based on this questionnaire I'm about to fill out?"

My daring side-eye warned the host he'd better not lie to me.

Chuckling, he sat my empty glass at the corner of the desk and stepped behind it. "That about sums it up, but we like to think of it as a short-term dating service without all the false pretenses and long drawn out periods of fake pleasantries most people hate."

Isn't that the truth?

He handed me a tablet and a stylus.

"The questionnaire asks a lot of personal questions, but they will help you two get a good snapshot of each other's lives. For security purposes, you don't supply your name or any personally identifiable information that can be tracked.

"You and your selection will use this facility for a private meeting, which will include a massage. All of our members are certified massage therapists. The massage meet-and-greet is where you will decide on the time, place, and activities you'd like to set up for your date. We've had couples go sky diving and even jetting across the country on a night to remember. You can also choose to keep things simple and meet here in one of our luxury suites after your massage."

I blinked at the man, not responding at first. "I know you said it already, but I need to hear it one more time. I get to sample the meat. I can do more than touch it?"

He pointed at the tablet. "Your choice has listed all that he will and won't do. He has even provided a copy of his medicals that have been sanitized of all identifying personal information so that you can feel comfortable knowing that you're with someone who is healthy. Since you have decided to move to the next step, we do require you to provide your medicals as soon as possible. Are they easily assessable?"

"Yes, I can retrieve a copy and email it to you from my phone."

"If you'll please give me your phone number, I'll send you our secure link for you to upload your information. We have to verify its authenticity before we sanitize it for your selection's viewing."

"So, someone here will see my information?"

He nodded.

"I can assure you that we'll safeguard your medical paperwork as we would our own records. We have never had an identity leak, and we have been around for a decade."

"Okay," I replied, believing him. Was I really about to go through with this? The little drunk voice in the back of my mind said, *"Fucking right, you are!"*

"I'm going to go and make sure the room is prepared for your massage," the host announced, standing.

After acknowledging him with a quick nod, I resumed my task of filling out the questionnaire. Glossing over the answers my meat selection had provided, I noticed that there wasn't much he wasn't willing to do sexually.

This whole process made my blood flow faster while the situation's overwhelming heaviness chewed at my nerves to even me out. I hit send on a snapshot of my medical paperwork and filled out the questionnaire, diving farther into this world.

This was a once in a lifetime chance, and I was willing to keep an open mind as long as the activities weren't hazardous to my health.

CHAPER FOUR

Camina

"The room is ready," the host announced when he stepped back into the office. He took the tablet and with a few clicks, shipped the questionnaire off to wherever it had to go before extending his hand to escort me to the treatment room.

We walked across the dim display room, but instead of taking a left back to the reception area, we turned right onto a hall that led us deeper into 'The Market.'

The relaxing scent of lavender had me taking in deep, eye-closing breaths. The temperature was that perfect cool, just before cold. A number of strategically-placed wall-mounted monitors showed you shimmering ocean views and leaves fluttering in the wind against a summer sky.

We passed what I assumed were treatment rooms, one on each side of the hallway, before stopping at the last door on the right. I stepped into the room, and the host followed.

"When you're ready, all you have to do is push this button." He pointed out a small white button near the door. "Then, disrobe, lay face down on the massage table, and place your face in the donut."

A quick nod was my reply because my body was humming with charged energy at the notion of being touched by actual human hands. Knowing the hands of the man with the dream dick would be massaging me had nasty thoughts being dragged through every gutter in my mind, and there were many.

I removed everything except my panties and tied myself into the fluffy white robe before picking up the tablet to highlight the areas I wanted massaged. After highlighting every body part available on the screen, I pressed the ready button, hung up my robe, and climbed atop the massage table. Twisting and turning, I worked myself under the sheets, pulled on the therapeutic sleep mask they had sitting at the head of the table, and placed my face into the donut.

The tunes spilling into the room and the soothing scents all worked in keeping me relaxed. I had fallen into such a deep state of relaxation that I lost time, so the door opening jarred me and my body automatically tensed.

"Relax," a male voice sounded, the tone low but strong. One word and it gave me a full description of the seductively tempting timbre in his voice. Although I had a sheet covering me, his hand pressing into my lower back without warning made me jump.

"You indicated you enjoy strong pressure, but I'll start with medium, and you tell me if it's too much because I have a tendency of going deep, too deep, I'm told."

Oh shit! With what he was working with down below, he wasn't being arrogant.

"Okay," I answered, my voice breathy. He went through the task of feeling out the contours of my body through the sheets, lingering in the most stressed areas. He adjusted my sheets, tucking them so that my back was exposed. He then placed my arms so they would relax and hang off the sides of the table.

I could hear him squeezing oil into his hands before rubbing them together with loud wet swipes that sounded sexual.

"We aren't obligated to give names, but I noticed on your questionnaire that you would like to be called Mystery."

His strong fingers pressing into my knotted shoulders stopped my reply, and I sucked in a satisfying breath instead.

"Why did you choose Mystery?" he questioned.

"Because outside of all the information I fed into that questionnaire, you will never truly know who I am. I'll always be a mystery to you, and so will you to me."

"Well, Mystery, I hope by the time we're done, I'll have picked up enough clues to solve the case," he said in a husky tone while pressing my shoulders into the vice of his strong hands. The delicious squeeze had me breathing hard as his masculine scent and the light mist of his cologne broke through the lavender atmosphere and invaded my senses.

"Too much?" he asked.

"I like a touch of pain," I told him, aware it sounded sexual.

"Good. I like giving it," he replied, lifting the sheets as he circled the table, running warm hands up each part of my body he revealed.

"I must compliment you. You have a beautiful body. Tense, but sexy." The pitch in his tone was so heavy it felt like his words were dragging along my skin.

"Thank you," I replied. "I'm a mechanic by trade, so that helps, but I also work out at least three times a week. I'm over thirty and unmarried, and although I feel youthful, my family and friends treat me like an old maid. And the fact that I can't find a decent man even if one sat on my lap adds to my need to preserve my youth."

"I can assure you, a woman as beautiful as you doesn't have anything to worry about. You are an exquisite gift to the senses, and any man who doesn't appreciate your efforts is a damn fool."

He was making me blush, and it took a moment to speak through the deep smile he'd put on my face.

"I appreciate that," I replied, not giving a damn if he was offering false flattery because I was eating that shit up.

His oily hands were moving down my back, making a wet-sliding sound with more firmness this time. Those hands and the added pressure stirred something that hadn't been stirred in any of my previous massages.

"Oh," I breathed when his thumb pressed into a knot at the top of my left shoulder. My reaction spurred him to keep the pressure going. He massaged me so well and firmly, I had to fight to keep from moaning.

"So, Mystery. Will you be continuing to the final step?"

"Mmm," escaped before I could stop it. "I've never done this or anything close to it, so will you tell me what usually happens?" I asked.

"Normally, after I'm chosen, I give a massage, we talk, and set a meet location for later in the evening, or sometimes we meet here at 'The Market,' so that we can take care of the things mentioned on the questionnaire."

His words had me wanting to know what that dream dick of his would feel like on and in other parts of my body.

"Mystery," he called. His tone was back to that husky timbre, now that his hands were at my lower back and sinking into the dimples I had above my butt cheeks.

"Yes," I answered in a lazy drawl. Had he asked something? His magic hands had me floating.

"Can I make a suggestion?" he offered, putting an end to my search for where we were in the conversation.

"Sure," I replied.

"I'd like to do something a little more traditional than usual?"

A laughed bubbled up to the surface, tickling my throat. "I'm sorry, but there is nothing about this that could remotely qualify as traditional."

I inhaled deeply before releasing a satisfying sigh. He was still at my lower back, sucking out the tension there through the hard press of his fingertips while also flirting with the tops of my ass cheeks.

"I do want to hear your suggestion, but will you answer a question for me first?"

"Yes," he replied before adding the hard pressure from his strong palm that I liked.

"Mmm," I didn't hide my moan this time as my tongue skated across my lips. "Why do you do this if not for financial gain?"

A series of fast-moving and rotating presses in my flank area had my eyes rolling in my head.

"For those of us who are not ready for a long-term relationship, this is a fast-paced and effective way to meet, date, and move on without strings being attached. It's exclusive for one night, so we've had very few problems with the process. Since there is no exchange of contact information, it makes the process that much smoother."

"I can see the appeal. I ended my last relationship nearly three years ago, and all I felt was relief. I get lonely, often, but I remind myself of all the time I wasted on something that wasn't going anywhere. And dating…" I huffed. "Dating is a joke, and I'm beginning to think that it's a curse too."

He chuckled.

"We have a female version of this type of market if you'd like to become a member. Some of our members have met their better half dating this way."

My loud laugh had my body bouncing. "You call this dating?"

"Yes. You find out more about a person this way *and* much faster. We've reviewed each other's profiles, and less than thirty percent of it is sexual if you hadn't noticed."

Favorite colors, foods, hobbies, and everything needed to pack a lifetime into twenty-four hours had populated that questionnaire. I'd also picked up enough clues to know that this man had a stressful job as a high-level business executive.

"So, this is like speed dating on meth with a heavy dose of physical interaction? Based on that questionnaire alone, I believe you know more about me than the man I spent three years with."

He was above my flank area, driving his palms into the tightness there and making me forget what I'd said last.

"Would you be interested in being a member?" he asked again and paused, waiting for my reply.

"Heck, no. I can't do this. No offense, but I don't think I can put myself on display to be picked by a strange man who only wants to fuck me and move on."

Did I just offend him? Thinking better of it, I didn't believe anyone who had the balls to do something like this would be easily offended.

"How old are you? How long have you been doing this? How long do you plan to do it?" I questioned.

"I'll be forty in a few months. I've been doing this for three years. I travel a great deal for work, so dating this way works for me. 'The Market' has locations in the cities I visit, so I'm rarely without company. This works well for me, *for now*."

"You make this type of *dating* sound appealing, but it's like having an in-depth one-night stand. What if you never get picked from the line-up? What if you're not attracted to the woman that picks you? How long do you go at this before you find yourself wanting something more?"

It sounded like I was interrogating the man.

"A part of the thrill for us is being in the line-up. We all get picked at least two to four times a month, and there are other activities I devote my time to outside 'The Market.' One of the qualifications of being a member is to have an open mind about women. However, I must admit, I did cheat this time because I was the one who gave you the card last week."

I gasped and jerked my head up, although the mask covering my eyes blinded me.

"You were sitting in the booth behind me?" The question came out as a harsh whisper. "How did you know when I'd be here or that I'd show at all? Also, there was no guarantee that I'd choose you. What if I'd chosen someone else?"

"Like I said, I cheated. All of us in the area received a notification when you swiped your card in the front door. However, last week, I gave the host your description and asked him to send me an extra alert whenever you came in. I live near, so when he texted, I came. If you hadn't picked me, I was prepared to bribe or do whatever else it took to see you again."

Was he serious?

"Also, that night at the restaurant, I empathized with parts of your conversation and believed you deserved this unique experience. It wasn't until after I left the restaurant that I realized I wanted you to experience it with me."

Why me?

"I'm flattered. Thank you," I replied in a breathy tone, failing not to sound enamored. How could this man whose face I'd never seen make me feel so special? Was I reading too much into this situation?

We grew quiet after that. Him likely thinking about the freaky shit I'd agreed to on the questionnaire and me about what he'd just revealed. He moved back to my shoulders, kneading with the perfect amount of pressure that made my useless thoughts disappear. This was a one night stand. There was no need for me to overthink it.

"That feels good," I purred out loud, not intending to but unable to help myself.

"Good. How's this?" he asked, making tight circles with his thumbs.

"Even better," I replied, not caring anymore that his massage had me moaning like we were having sex and getting wet like he was dishing out foreplay. Was I supposed to be getting aroused?

He kept at it, adding more firmness to the pressure points that apparently had a direct connection to my erogenous zones. Zaps of lust traveled to my pussy, making it pulse with life. If he kept it up, he was about to catch a whiff of my arousal. My lack of sight heightened the erotic sensations rolling through me and made me squirm.

"I'm sorry, but," I moaned, breathless. "If you keep that up..." panting now.

"Let me pleasure you. It's all I've wanted to do since I heard and sneaked distorted peeks at you at that restaurant. I want you to remember me." He cleared his throat. "I want you to remember this experience."

I would remember it all right. A series of quick breaths escaped, making my chest push against the table. There was nothing I could do now to hide that he had me riding a burning desire, strong enough to let go of my inhibitions.

He kept working my pressure points while placing his soft lips against my ear. His warm breath teased my lobe and sent a warm thrill rushing through me.

"I want to hear what you sound like when you come," he whispered.

"Oh. God," my voice came out in a rushed whisper while I fought to breathe and grasp the fact that I was about to—

"Shit. I'm com...ing." My body shook and shivered shamelessly, causing the table to make creaking sounds while I moaned through my unexpected orgasm, the strongest I'd had in a while.

"Dayum," I breathed before biting into my bottom lip. "Mmm," I moaned, savoring the explicit joy rolling through me and feeling the pulse in my pussy jumping like I'd had penetration sex. *What the hell?*

Once I stopped shaking, I laid there, stunned, my mind in a thousand places at once.

"I'm sorry," was all I could think to say.

"For what?" He leaned down and placed light kisses to my back, the soft pecks more caring than sexual.

"Don't apologize for any pleasure that I bring you. You allowed yourself to relax enough to absorb my touch fully. It means that you trust me enough to let your guard down even though you've never seen me. I believe we're going to have a wonderful time together."

Wasn't *that* the understatement of the century? His strokes were light now, soothing and relaxing.

"Was that okay, Mystery?"

I love the way he called me Mystery, even though it wasn't my real name. He said it with so much desire, like he wanted to discover all my secrets. A lighthearted schoolgirl giggle sounded, a sound that rarely came from me. "Are you kidding with that question? After the massage you just blessed me with," I replied, finally answering his question with one of my own.

He chuckled. "Believe me, the pleasure is all mine. Will you let me give you pleasure in other ways?"

Fucking right I will. I could sense his eyes roaming my body. The shit had my nipples tightening even while pressed into the firm cushion of the massage table. At this point, only the bottom half of my ass was covered by the sheet. This man knew about my piss-poor dating life and that my ass was a closet freak based on that questionnaire. There was no use lying now.

"Yes, you can bring me pleasure in other ways, but only if you let me do the same for you."

"Yes. I'd like that," he said in a tone so lust-heavy, the syllables dragged like he had trouble carrying them.

"You reviewed my questionnaire, but I need to give you a verbal warning about what I like." That statement got my full attention.

"I thrive on control, and my sexual tastes, as you read, are not traditional. I don't do vanilla sex."

"Okay," I replied, knowing damn well I should tell him I didn't know what half that shit on his questionnaire had meant.

"If you'll agree, I'd like to leave you an address for us to meet tomorrow evening. I'd like to cook you dinner and have some nice wine, even a movie if you're up for it. The rest of the night, we can *play*."

"It sounds too good to be true. You wouldn't get my hopes up and stand me up, would you?"

His warm, soft lips skimmed my neck and sat at my earlobe.

"It's taking every bit of willpower I have not to flip you over and fuck you right here and now. I can almost taste your arousal on my tongue. I can't wait to see how open I can get that pussy and how deep you can take my dick down your throat."

My hard swallow failed to choke down my whimper, and I couldn't help squirming as the flow of my arousal started up again and leaked between my jittery legs. The sound of his deep sniff filled the silence.

"I want nothing more than to spank that lush ass of yours raw for making me want you so fucking badly," he stated, speaking through clenched teeth. "I'll leave the address and instructions on the desk for you." His words were heavy and hasty, hinting that he was on the verge of fucking me as he'd stated. "Acknowledge my statement," he demanded.

I nodded, so breathless, it was difficult to utter clear words. The sexual tension in the room was so thick it had muddled my brain.

"Yes," I finally spit out.

He stepped back, taking all that masculine power with him. My senses were so heightened, I could hear the pen scraping across the pad he wrote on. A long silence followed, and I could sense his eyes on me.

"Tomorrow at six."

"Tomorrow at six," I repeated like the man had hypnotized me.

With that, he left, his steps sounding until he pulled the door closed behind him.

Relief washed over me, and my body relaxed into the table before I exhaled a deep breath.

What the hell had I agreed to?

CHAPTER FIVE

Camina

Reminiscent of my visit to 'The Market,' reluctance attempted to stifle my movement as I hopped out of the Uber at the entrance of another luxurious high-rise. I paid my fare with a few taps to my phone while strolling towards the building that housed some of the most expensive penthouses in the city.

I held the white key card and the note with his address and instructions between my fingers. Number one on the list had suggested I familiarize myself with the term BDSM. I'd fallen asleep and awakened with an obsessive need to soak up a culture I was clueless about. It didn't help matters that I had inadvertently volunteered myself to be a part of the lifestyle when I let my inner freak take the lead while filling out that questionnaire.

The interior of the elegantly-adorned lobby sparkled like new money, captivating enough to push away the disturbing images of me being tied to a St. Andrew's Cross and left in the middle of the Southwest Freeway.

Instead of letting doubt peck at my nerves, I strutted across the expansive lobby like I owned the place, tossing a wave at the two front desk attendants as though I knew them. Thanks to my military background, I knew how to rein in the confidence I needed while at the same time, praying for my feet in these heels and hoping I looked as sexy as I felt in my black zip-back dress. I'd taken the time and flat-ironed my hair which had been a jungle of tangled shoulder-length tresses a few hours ago.

After entering the elevator, I put in the required pin number, hit 25, and exhaled relief when the doors closed without a hitch. I exited the elevator a moment later, thinking I'd be entering a hall. Instead, I ended up facing a stylishly furnished foyer, leading to a set of open glass front doors.

The view from the doorway was a large, captivating living room that seemed to be straight from the pages of an Elle Décor magazine. I wasn't sure if I was supposed to announce my arrival or step inside. Was this his real home, or had he rented this place for our *date*?

"Please, come in," he called from the back. The sound of his voice traveled across the expansive living room and tickled my skin. I walked in, unable to keep myself from seeking out my first glimpse of *him*. He strolled into the living room, and the first sight froze me in place.

My legs had become two slabs of cement. The slow rise of my eyes captured every detail down to the pleat running up his stylish dark slacks and the rolled sleeves of his light blue pinstriped button-up.

The full visual confirmation of him was a relief counteracted by stress. Relieved because he was sexy as sin and stressful because he was a part of a world I'd never experienced based on his reveals in that questionnaire.

"Hello again," he greeted.

I think I spoke back as my gaze traced his clean-shaven, well-defined jawline and inched up to his lips. The sight of him flooded my bloodstream and provided a smooth, intoxicating warmth like the most expensive Bordeaux.

He flashed a set of flawless white teeth, surrounded by deep pink and kiss inducing lips. His nose was prominently-set in place and the rest of him a meticulously crafted work of art. He was handsome, verging on beautiful, if not for a small scar that marred the left side of his face along his lower jaw. His short, dark hair gleamed with a healthy shine that made me want to run my fingers through it.

Those eyes told a story of sexual domination wrapped in a package of masculine beauty. A lethal blue, they sparked electricity and tugged on something urgent at the deepest reaches of my being.

"Welcome to my home," he greeted, answering one of my questions and causing three more to develop. "You are beautiful," he complimented before letting his gaze rake leisurely over every inch of me.

The dress stopped just above my knees, not too sexy, but giving a peek of cleavage and pointing out the shape of my body. The black heels were sleek and sexy in their own right, and although they were murdering my poor feet, I made the sacrifice.

He didn't stop his approach until he was standing a foot away, breathing in the quick breaths I released.

"Dinner is almost ready. Would you like a glass of wine until then?" he asked. If the grin on his face was any indication, he meant his earlier compliment and loved what he saw. Turning, he placed his hand on the small of my back to move me away from the front door.

"Yes," I forced myself to reply to his wine offer. "I can help with finishing up dinner," I added, preferring to keep moving rather than drool over him. He was fine, sexy, and the sight of him alone had my damn hormones up and running wild. My pussy had its own heartbeat, and my nipples could make diamonds jealous they were so hard. This was a good sign because I hadn't felt these urges for the last five dates I'd been on.

His head tilted in agreement at my offer to help. "I'd like that. All I have left to prepare is our starter, the spinach-apple salad. I made one of your favorites, creamy lobster risotto, that we'll have with white wine, pearl onions, and green peas."

I walked into his kitchen, stopping at the counter where he was slicing an apple to add to the salad. The heavenly aroma of the lobster made my nostrils flare as I breathed it in, and the glass-top pot gave me a peek at the simmering rice. It was becoming clear that the questionnaire had worked.

While he uncorked the bottle of wine on the far counter, I busied myself by first washing my hands before picking up the knife he'd used to finish slicing the apple. Despite us both keeping busy, our eyes kept straying back to each other.

Small talk did nothing to stave off the lust making the pulse in my lady parts hum a sexy tune, *"I'm going to get some dick tonight, dick-dick-dick, tonight."*

Shut up! I forced the crazy tune from my head and noticed he had no trouble letting his eyes tell me how much he enjoyed watching me. They roamed, the intense heat in them scorching my skin and burning down to the bone.

It was hard to keep my tongue from sliding over my lips because my mind kept flipping through the Rolodex of positions I wanted him to put me in. The vision where my legs were pinned open by his muscled arms while my pussy gave his mouth sloppy kisses was the one that made my mouth go dry.

The food he'd prepared was tasty, but my taste buds were primed for a sample of something else, something that I knew was *piping hot, flavorful, and delicious*. My gaze dropped to the area that was hidden behind the table, and he noticed, flashing me an arrogant smirk.

"This is delicious," I stated, distracting myself by pointing at the meal and taking a sip of wine. He shoved his half-eaten plate of food away and tossed his linen over it.

"I think we're done," he forcibly announced. My gaze lifted from his discarded meal to meet his waiting eyes, fixed on me with a coat of lust so heavy, they dragged over my body. Following his lead, I shoved my plate away and finished off the wine in my glass with a hardy gulp.

"Yes. Looks like we are done."

He stood, making the chair grunt with his quick movement. "The way you're looking at me says you'd like to skip the movie too."

It wasn't a question, and if my teeth sank any deeper into my bottom lip, it would start bleeding. There was no need to be coy now. I'd come for the dick.

"What movie?" I asked with an expressionless face.

He chuckled, rounding the table before reaching for my hand and tugging a little to get me to stand. When we bypassed the living room, I assumed we were going to his bedroom until he stopped at the first door on the dimly-lit hallway. He keyed in a six-digit pin before the door popped open.

A deep crease lined my forehead while my eyes bounced between him and the door. Why did he need a pin number to get into a room inside his house?

"Lights," he called out when he pushed the door open and stood at the threshold, ushering his hand for me to enter first. My breath caught at the first sight of the space. It was triple the size of a standard room but was the furthest thing from a normal bedroom that I'd ever seen.

"Welcome to my dungeon. I call it, Wicked Truth."

Fitting name. There would be no lying to yourself in this room if you had wicked fantasies. I was about to find out if I had the balls to see my sexual daydreams become a reality. The wall to my right was all glass that allowed the twinkling city view to peek in.

However, the city view was forgotten because my attention was on the room's interior set up. The wall before me was an elaborate display of restraints, bit gags, dildos, cuffs, ropes, collars, muzzles, nipple clamps, butt plugs, and on and on.

There wasn't a piece of normal furniture in the entire room. A cage, spanking bench, and queening chair greeted. These were items I was clueless about a day ago. The bed was equipped with floor to ceiling bondage suspension gear, and the St. Andrew's Cross that had entered my mind when I'd walked into the building earlier sat in a cozy corner.

"This room hasn't been used in three years, so when I read your questionnaire, you have no idea how excited it made me. It's been thoroughly cleaned, and all of the hand-held toys are new," he said, not hiding the excitement brimming in his tone. "And, I'm certified in shibari," he added.

"I have no idea what that means," I said in a low tone, continuing to take in his *Wicked Truth* and attempting to figure out if I was scared or excited.

"Shibari means that I can tie, bound, and immobilize any part of your body using many types of rope or material with artistic precision and safety."

I nodded. When I was filling out that questionnaire yesterday, it was more about *envisioning* this type of fantasy versus actually fulfilling it. Looking at this scene, live and in person, was a cold slap of reality, and the longer I was in it, the more it hyped-up my starving libido.

"Are you a dominant, a Dom?" I questioned.

"Yes," he replied.

"Why me? I'm sure you've figured out by now that I've never done this. I allowed my curiosity to get the better of me when I was looking over your questionnaire. Besides, I thought Dom's had subs at their beck and call."

"When I need to, I visit one of the clubs I belong to. I do performances and often have extended engagements with a sub or two, so my needs in that department are being met."

"Is this where you use sex and domination to brainwash me until you turn me into your personal sex slave?"

He shrugged, and a devilish smirk sat prominently on his face.

"I don't need you to submit *to me*, per se, but to submit to your own desires. You will simply give me what I need by allowing me to give *you* what *you* desire."

He ran a strong hand up my arm before I could process his statements fully. The action had me glancing deeper into his demanding gaze.

"No matter how perverse you may think something is, if it turns you on, kicks up your pulse, puckers your nipples, or gets that pussy wet, then enjoy it, give in to it, embrace it."

His damn words were as much a turn on as this sexed-up room. He stood me in the center of the room before he started circling my body, inspecting me.

"You are a fucking sexy woman," he replied, more to himself than me, so I didn't respond but stood under the weight of his gaze. My pulse hammered faster, and the beat was drumming in my ears when he stopped in front of me.

"Since this is your first time, we won't get into anything too hardcore. We're going to play a game, so listen to the rules carefully. If anything is too uncomfortable, painful, or stressful, you let me know immediately."

"Okay," I replied because I somehow read in his expression that he demanded a verbal response.

"Rule one: From now until the game ends, you're to address me as Sir. Every answer, question, or comment will start or end with Sir." He held up two fingers. "Rule two: When you want to or need to come, you ask me first. Do it without my permission, and I'll find a way to punish you." I swallowed hard to digest his second rule. "Rule three: Beg. What I'm about to give you is invaluable, so if you want to keep receiving it, you fucking beg me for it like it's the only thing that will keep you alive. This game can last five minutes, or it can last all night, but it depends solely on your responses and how well you remember the rules. You understand?"

"Yes, sir," I replied.

A growl sounded, and his blue eyes had gone dark with ravenous intent. "The fact that I didn't have to remind you to say *Sir* has my fucking dick hard. You keep this up, and I may have to put you in that sling so you can get first-hand knowledge of *my* definition of a hard fuck."

If a few words from my lips could do that to him, I couldn't imagine what the physical stuff would do. The rules sounded simple enough. Besides, my freak was peeking out, and the horny bitch was ready to play.

"There is trust between us, it was proven in the treatment room, but it's not strong enough for me to push your boundaries *too hard* unless I believe you can take it. Good thing for you, I'm *very good* at reading body language."

I swallowed, wishing I had another glass of wine. He continued his inspection, lingering behind me so long that the hairs on the back of my neck stood on end and made the muscles in my shoulders tighten.

"I'm going to repeat this because I place your safety above all else. If anything becomes too much, too tight, too uncomfortable, too hard, or too painful, I need you to tell me."

"Yes, Sir," I replied before lifting a brow and swallowing a thick lump of, *oh shit*. Were we really about to do this? Once he'd finished making me squirm, he stood before me, his six-two frame towering over my minuscule five-five.

"I hate hearing the word no, and I don't like using safe words as I prefer to read body language. However, you deserve a little gift for your first time, so you can consider the word 'no' as good as your safe word tonight. Understand?"

"Yes, Sir. I understand."

"Can I kiss you?" he asked.

"Yes, Sir," rolled off my lips *way* too fast.

He took a lingering step that put him so close that the warmth emanating from him poured over me like melted caramel. He leaned in with a demanding magnetism that made me go still as his gaze remained locked on mine. His lips pressed over mine with an assured softness that enticed me to lean into his strong body, but I fought the impulse and held my position. Something about this man stilled and held me captive, both mentally and physically. Like getting that chill when you knew danger was lurking. Was there such a thing as *good* danger?

He deepened the kiss before taking a possessive tug on my lips, first the top and then the bottom. I attempted but failed to choke down a relieving sigh, not even sure if it was allowed.

My lips parted for his strong wet tongue. The slick sensation of it stroking mine sent aching spikes of need straight to my head before falling lower and adding spice to the pulsing in my pussy.

"Can I touch those pretty nipples that have been calling out for attention?" I didn't know what my body was doing, but if he wanted to touch it, I sure as shit wasn't going to say no.

"Yes, Sir," I answered as he reached around me before closing me into his masculine warmth to unzip my dress. My eyes closed the moment I breathed in his spicy hot scent. He unzipped my dress and slipped it down my body with the swiftness of a professional burglar. He glanced up, pinning his gaze to mine while holding the dress at my feet for me to step out of before tossing it *somewhere*.

He followed up his action by standing and reaching behind me to unsnap my strapless bra with a quick flick of his fingers. My hormones were revved so high, I didn't care that I was standing there in nothing but my heels and panties.

The delicious peck he placed on my lips felt like a reward before he dipped his head to meet my puckered nipples. He blew on my left nipple and placed a gentle kiss on the right. It had been a while since I'd had any good foreplay, so I was soaking this up like a sponge.

He continued asking for permission to kiss and lick certain areas, my stomach, belly button, and so on. "Yes, Sir," were the only words in my head, and I was starting to understand how one could become programmed. With the amount of attention the two words were getting me, I'd say them with pride.

My gaze followed his everchanging motions. It was like he had planned ahead to conquer me. I watched him drag my soaking wet panties down my legs, eye-fucking me the entire time.

Once he had my panties off, he didn't toss them like he had my dress. He lifted them to his nose and took a deep eye-closing sniff, cupping the thin red fabric in his hand like it was a precious gem.

He seemed enraptured by my scent—his body appearing to fold around his hand as he remained in his lowered position, breathing in my soaked panties like he was praying to them.

"I could get high off your essence," he stated. His heavy gaze made it appear that he was already buzzed.

"I'm starving for a taste of that pussy," he stated, keeping my panties to his nose as he eyeballed my clean-shaven mound, shaking his head purposefully and slowly.

"I'm going to shove my tongue so far up your pussy, it's going to teach your g-spot how to talk." With words that bold, I believed him. He lifted his blaring gaze onto mine, the look making my heart do its best to claw its way out of my chest. "You better beg like hell to keep me going. Think you'll have a problem begging for it?"

My tongue got stuck to the roof of my dry mouth, and I sputtered, "No, no Sir," while shifting and attempting to quiet my throbbing clit.

Teasing tickles of his tongue lapped at the inside of my right thigh and kept my juices leaking like he was calling them to the surface. He caught a line of the flowing wet heat trailing down my leg and traced it back up with the tip of his finger. He sucked hard on his wet digit before he stood, took my hand, and led me to a bench that resembled a cross folded at a ninety-degree angle with an extended headrest.

I was positioned against the cushioned planks meant for my legs, and he tapped against my inner thighs to get my legs spread and aligned. "Bend over," he ordered, and I eagerly complied. The curve of the equipment was taller than my waist, so I had to stand on my tiptoes, even in heels, in order to arch over properly.

The position left my ass and pussy wide open to him. I assumed I'd feel self-conscious, but when you'd been starving for sexual attention for as long as I have, modesty wasn't high on the priority list. Thankfully, I'd had the presence of mind to do a bikini wax after I'd left 'The Market' yesterday. If he'd seen the Chia Pet that was growing down there, I doubt he'd be so eager to touch my pussy.

"Spread your legs wider," he growled from behind me. I swore I felt the heat of his passion smack me on the ass from his sexually charged tone. He widened the spreader bar on the floor to keep my legs apart and proceeded to lock restraints around my ankles to anchor me to the bench.

His movements were slow as he paced around me, no doubt checking his handiwork. He reached for my hands, and I gave them, eager to find out if he would fulfill his promise to bury his tongue in my pussy.

He tugged my hands so that my arms spread wide and flat against the surface of the planks, stretching my body so that I was off balance in my heels and teetering on the balls of my feet. He closed the thick leather straps around one wrist and repeated the process with the other, not leaving me much wiggle room. The restraints had me stretched tight and bent at the waist in a perfect L shape with the back of my body fully exposed and at his mercy.

Why did being restrained and helpless excite me? Why did the knowledge that he could do what he wanted spike a fearful level of excitement within me that made my lust boil hotter? The fiery sensations coursing through my blood was a type of foreplay that was turning me on like nothing else ever had.

"Do you have a problem with me tapping that delicious ass?" he questioned. A smile spread across my face while I stared into the twinkling city view pouring in through the windows. I didn't know if anyone could see us, and the fact that I hadn't asked was telling of how high my lust levels had risen.

I bit into my smile and finally answered his question. "No, Sir."

CHAPTER SIX

Colson

The deliciously round ass displayed before me had me fighting to wipe out images of plunging my dick, balls deep, into Mystery's tight little pussy hole. I wanted her so badly that she was making me forget she was a novice.

With great reluctance, I walked away from her, causing her to snap her head up as her wide gaze followed my every move. The intoxication of my awareness for her was a steady stream of hot energy coursing through my veins while I stood with my back to her and observed the assortment of paddles and riding crops.

"You assumed when I asked if I could tap that ass, I was talking about sex?" I questioned her without turning around. Her steady breaths were flowing like liquid lust was being sprayed into the air. "Ye...Yes, Sir," she answered.

"I'm not that easy, baby. I'm going to make you work for this dick," I told her, loving the sound of the little gasp she released. Her eyes grew wide at the sight of my dick jumping behind the material of my pants.

Picking up a 29" black leather riding crop, I whirled it through the air before slapping it against the inside of my palm while keeping my eyes on Mystery's big unblinking ones. Although I was sure she'd never been spanked, I sensed that she would love it.

The way her breaths quickened, it wasn't hard to guess that the sight of the crop and what I intended to do with it was turning her on. I'd bet that pussy was already flowing with anticipation.

I stepped around her, enjoying the picture of sexual perfection she presented laid across my spanking bench with that fine ass in the air and clean-shaven pussy on display. I stilled my movements, allowing silence to fall into the scene. Its lingering stillness had her body a mess with anxious jerks, adding fuel to her anticipation.

"This is my first time starting with a spanking, but with you, I sense that you need this more than I need to baby you about this lifestyle."

Her heavy breaths filled the dungeon as she laid her cheek against the bench. Her sexy body visibly tightened in preparation for what was to come.

"May I use this crop to spank you?" I asked, knowing what her answer would be. As long as I heard yes, I'd keep going as far as she would allow me to take her down the rabbit hole of sinful deeds.

"Yes, Sir." Her words were a breathy murmur. I waited longer this time, allowing the silence to linger long enough for her body to release some of her coiled tension.

Thwat!

I delivered the first solid blow. The crop's wide popper connected square across both cheeks.

"Aww!" she yelled out. Her body tightened, and she tugged hard against the restraints. The fully exposed sight of her naked round ass had me swallowing lust so fast, I was in fear of choking on it. Eventually, she'd notice that the sound of the spanks was more intimidating than the sting.

Thwat! Thwat!

Two more licks were delivered harder this time, making her mouthwatering cheeks bounce from the impact. She writhed with a mix of shock from the peppery ache and a straining desire for more. The sound of the hard leather connecting with her firm, silky flesh sent zings of sick satisfaction coursing through me.

I delivered three more lashes that prompted a gasp and started the flow of her hot juices. It was like watching fresh nectar dripping from a peach, and the scent had me closing my eyes to savor the enticing aroma. The deep press of her teeth into her bottom lip, as she poked her ass out for more, showed she liked it, like I knew she would.

"Do you want more?"

"Yes, Sir," she answered in a rush. "Please," she begged, dragging the word out and remembering the rules like a fucking champ. When I just stood there, not giving her what she wanted, she looked back, her body twitching. "Please, Sir. Can I have some more?"

"Good girl," I said, knowing that she was getting into the right subspace. Four spanks, hard and fast, connected all over that beautiful ass, leaving colorful, fleshy marks like paint splashes on a perfect brown canvas. Her body ached for more so badly that her inner thighs trembled. Her quivering flesh and her hard, heaving breaths were a distracting combo.

"Tonight is all about you getting a live sneak peek into the life. Should I keep going?"

"Yes, Sir. Please. Please keep going," she replied harshly, saying more with the deep dip she'd put in her back than she was with her words. I wanted her begging harder, but I couldn't deny the way her body burned with a sexual need so strong that the heat she gave off licked at my skin and sparked my dark passion. Her conversation from the restaurant resurfaced, reminding me of how much need she was in. The poor woman was sexually starving.

I delivered swat after swat, pausing to make her beg and enjoying the way her muscles worked against the pulling tension of her body. Anticipation and satisfaction were in competition based on her deep moans that filled the dungeon, giving it life and spilling her truth.

"Sir, I think I'm about to...I mean, can I..." She muttered through heavy moans. I bet she was running those rules I'd set through her head. I sent a series of light taps against her ass to keep her right at the subspace she was starting to float into.

"Sir," she called. Her body was a mass of hard trembles. Her self-control was strong for someone who had never done this. "Yes," I answered, impressed and turned on by her will-power because it meant I could push her limits that much further. I tapped the crop harder, alternating against each cheek and making her work to keep from falling apart.

"May I, please—" she breathed hard and deeply. "Come?" She finally finished her question. Everything in me wanted to say no, but I had to keep reminding myself that she wasn't my sub, and this was her first time in the game. "Yes. Come, baby."

I gifted her two of the hardest spanks yet, the delicious sting making her back bow before she let go on a deep, relieved sigh. The invisible rush of release ricocheted through her, sending her into a frenzy of jerky movements like she was sizzling on a hot surface. I continued with light taps to her ass, keeping the flow of her orgasm rolling through her.

Her release created a beautifully harmonious song, a chorus of throaty moans and spasming movements that drew me in so smoothly, I was stroking her back before I realized it. The bench creaked and groaned against her shifting weight before she dissolved into a limp heap, the wrist restraints keeping her in place.

"You liked the way I spanked that ass, didn't you?" I continued to ease whatever sting was left with soothing strokes to her plump cheeks. She was still winded. "Yes, Sir." She managed to lift her head to answer my question before it fell like a weight back against the bench.

She released a strangled, "Oh shit," when I leaned down and sent my tongue gliding across the tender skin of each cheek, licking the sting away and revealing a little more of my wicked nature. She was one of the most receptive women I'd encountered in a long time, and I had nearly gotten off on getting *her* off.

"Look at the mess you've made. Should I clean you up?" Her head snapped up at my question as her heavy gaze reached across her shoulder and landed on mine. The idea of what I was asking planted itself in her head and made her eyes pop with renewed excitement.

She nodded before her tongue skated across her lips. "Yes, Sir. Please."

My exploring fingers ran along the backs of each delicious thigh before I stepped away to retrieve one of many fresh, wet towels I'd placed in various locations throughout the room. I cleaned her inner thighs, being careful not to take her nectar away from the delicate folds of her glistening lower lips.

Stooping behind her, put me eye level with her ass and exposed pussy. If I had my way, I'd make her my sub and train her so I could introduce her to every item in this room and take that virgin ass of hers. She couldn't see what I was doing, so the unknown caused her breath to pick up its winding cadence.

"Your lovely little pussy is so ripe and ready, just the way I like. Can I eat this soaked beauty?" I hardly heard her reply, "Yes, Sir," because I was fascinated by the sight of her silky wet flesh, driven by the citrus and honey scent she gave off, and salivating for a taste of her.

She hadn't even said please, and I didn't give a shit. I dived in, mouth first, lips connecting with lips while the juicy wet heat she released coated my hungry tongue and spread like lip gloss over my lips. Her flavor was a sweet and tangy blend that made me lick faster and roll my tongue over her pussy like a towelette wiping up spilled juice.

"You're fucking delicious," I mumbled before flicking my tongue up her clit, and using my fingers to spread her lips until I saw her inner walls pulsing. Her plush pink center eagerly greeted me, the quick beats of her pulse drumming against my tongue when I shoved it inside her quivering flesh.

I licked, sucked, and fucked her with my tongue and mouth. Plunging in from nose to chin, I was lost in the sexy roll of her body against my face and her riding my tongue as much as the restraints allowed. Her strangled cries and harsh breaths were back to an urgent shout where her heart was probably pounding against her ribs to get out of her chest.

Her loud moans were mixed with the hard yanking sounds she made pulling the restraints. I was afraid she'd snap the leather and metal holding her in place because her body was drawn so tightly. Only the balls of her feet and toes were inside her sexy black heels that wobbled and tapped against the floor.

However erratic her breaths and feet were, her body was fluid where she needed it to be because her wet heat drizzled over my tongue. She fed me her second orgasm, quelling the savage hunger within me.

"That's it, baby, give me what I helped to create, a delicious fucking orgasm." I commanded more from her while continuing to flick my tongue. The way her flavor shot through my system, her enchanting look, and her heat-seeking breaths had me about to start pleading with *her*.

When I finally removed my mouth from the hot and never-ending flow I had tapped into, I lavished her with tender tongue strokes along her back as she lay across the table like it was all that kept her from melting into a puddle.

I bent to undo her legs and found that I was unable to stop myself from running my hands along the silky surface of her calves that were toned enough to entice and soft enough to keep me stroking.

Once her ankles were released and the spreader bar removed, she did nothing to close her legs, maintaining the beautiful pose while I stepped around the front to undo her hands.

While I unbuckled her restraints, I glanced to see that she was already staring up at me. "Can I fuck you next?" I asked.

A hard swallow made her throat bob before a slow curiosity spread across her face. "Yes, Sir," she answered, her voice raspy from all that moaning and shouting she'd been doing.

I walked around to assist her by placing an arm securely under her shoulder to get her standing in those wobbly heels. She lifted slowly from the bent angle, reintroducing her body to the proper way it was supposed to function.

Once she was sure-footed, I escorted her to the foot of the bed. She cast a hard stare at the sling attached to the tall metal bars welded to the bed. Based on her pensive expression, she was no doubt attempting to figure out how the equipment would aid in our next adventure.

CHAPTER SEVEN

Camina

What kind of delicious torment was this man going to introduce me to next? Who knew I had this much freak in me? Apparently, *Sir* had the key to unlocking my inhibitions because this was his third time in two days to make me come without dick penetration.

Now, I was standing at the foot of his bed, attempting to unravel the sling and bench contraption he was about to put me in. He'd attached a sitting bench to the sling equipment, letting me know I wasn't ready to be fully slung. I suppose it was like a car seat for kinky beginners.

He was certified in this stuff, so I believed he knew best and based on the level of caution he'd used in getting everything prepared, there was no doubt that he took my safety seriously. The bench portion of the sling sat at his midsection and thick roped chains with leather bonds attached to the ends were swung from the top of the metal frames reaching high above us.

"Have a seat," he told me. I took the seat, and the cold leather pressing into my back, butt, and thighs reminded me of how comfortable I'd gotten in my nakedness. I'd all but forgotten that the heels were supposed to be hurting my feet.

The seat was tilted slightly upwards, so I laid back, glad that it sat tall enough for me to rest my head against. My feet hung over the sides, hovering above the floor.

"Relax," he said, flashing a devilish smirk at me anxiously eyeballing his every move. He reached above my shoulder and began cranking a knob that repositioned the seat farther back to forty-five degrees until I was able to look comfortably up at the ceiling. My gaze locked with the reflection of my own eyes in one of the mirrored sections in the ceiling.

"Hands above your head," he commanded. He dialed down the flaming heat in his eyes when his naughty gaze locked on mine. "Can I bind your wrist again?" he questioned.

"Yes, Sir," I answered. The fire I saw blazing in his eyes after my quick answer made my pulse pound with excitement, and my nerves clench in fear. He secured my arms above my head and shook them to test the restraints before stepping back.

"Can I have your left foot?" I lifted my leg, and only when I said, "Yes, Sir," did he take it, gripping the back of my ankle in his strong hands. He began by running his hand up the back of my leg until his fingers teased the bend of my knee. His hand rose higher until I began to understand what those intimidating thick metal chains with the restraints attached to them were for. The leathered portion of the binds was placed and wrapped around my upper thighs where his hands would go if he were fucking me in this position.

Holy fuck! What the hell had I gotten myself into with this man?

Once my legs were secure, I didn't think the positioning was so bad since there was plenty of slack left in the chains. However, my face bunched when he placed his hand against my stomach and reached above my shoulder.

"Can I lift your legs higher?" I nodded before whispering, "Yes, Sir," because my voice no longer worked with the large knot of anxiety I had swallowed. How high was he going to go?

He began cranking a lever that drew in the fat metal chains above and made them disappear into the sturdy poles they protruded from. My eyes kept shifting from the disappearing chains to my legs that were being raised higher and higher so that my knees were eye-level with my head. When the adjusting was done, my lower body had slid forward, giving him a tilted upward view of my pussy.

"Can I spread your legs? Wide?" he asked. I squeaked out my reply. "Yes, Sir." Fear had seeped in, laying claim to my lust and making me fight to maintain my composure. A loud metallic pop repeatedly sounded while he worked a lever that spread my legs to his satisfaction. The position he'd put me in gave him maximum exposure to *everything*.

"How flexible are you? Can I open you a little bit more?" I stared at him. If he opened me any further, I doubted my ass would remain on the bench seat, and he'd be able to look through my pussy and see through my eyes. I swallowed, remembering that a 'no' answer was like saying a safe word and would stop him from delivering what might be my best or worst sex ever. Thanks to the military, I didn't know how to quit once I started something, so I was determined to see what was in store for me.

"Yes, Sir," I answered with more bravery than I felt. Another loud pop made me jump, and as I'd suspected, the man had my bent legs lifted and spread so wide, my ass barely brushed the bench seat. If he wanted to, he could fuck me in the ass, and there wouldn't be shit I could do but take it. I was in a semi-slung position now with my back against the leather bench and more exposed than I had ever been in my life, even with my gynecologist.

I gave myself a once over before taking in the satisfied smirk on his face. His eyes were on my pussy that was leaking brazenly, despite the spikes of fear pinging through me. My nipples were puckered so tightly they stung. His tongue slid across his lips before he allowed his gaze to travel up my body until his eyes met mine.

"Don't worry, I'm going to make you come at least three times." At that promise, a low throaty moan escaped, and I didn't know if it was in fear or anticipation. If he fucked me in the position I was in, with the size he was packing, I was bound to be left with a permanent limp.

All it took to take my mind off my trussed up positioning was for him to take off his shirt. Toned muscles, firm pecs, and rigid abs were a gift to my sight. When he dropped those pants and reintroduced me to the meat I had selected, my hormones caught the holy ghost and jumped up and down my core. The sight of his dick made me forget all about my lower half being suspended by chains and my arms secured to the bench.

He stood before me, letting my hunger build at the sight of his beautifully big, thick dick. He stroked it up and down with slow-moving caresses and a firmness that made the head glisten and play peek-a-boo with me.

He reached out with his free hand and pinched one of my puckered nipples, but it wasn't his fingers doing the pinching. He'd smoothly fixed my tight flesh with a nipple clamp that gave a sharp but pleasing bite. Surprisingly, the hard pinch of the clamp eased the lingering sting that had been there.

The small, leash-like metal chain dangling from the clamp gave me pause until I noticed the other end of the chain had another clamp. He fastened my other nipple and let go of the shiny metal leash swinging between them. Now, one pull on the little leash and my nipples would be at his mercy.

He dropped lower, his tongue dragging down my stomach, and didn't stop until he'd flicked at my clit. Without stopping his exquisite tongue action, he eased in two long fingers, curving them to tickle my g-spot.

He moaned in eye-closing pleasure against my pussy like it was tonight's dessert before he let his stiff, lengthy tongue dip lower. "Oh! Fuck!" I yelled out. My damn inner thighs were shaking and making the metal chains sing a sex jingle.

The man had his fingers and his tongue in my pussy at the same time while his top lip was rubbing my clit. His actions made my eyes roll so far to the back of my head, it left my eyelids fluttering so that it appeared I was watching a strobe flicker.

"Sir!" I yelled.

"Yes. Come," he answered, knowing what his devilish ministrations were doing to me. His tongue and fingers worked with the sole purpose of ungluing me from reality. I came so hard the force of my pounding orgasm kept me in its tight grip before abruptly releasing me from its suffocating hold. I moaned and pulled uselessly against straps, chains, and the strong leather that held me captive.

Through my haze, I caught snapshots of him producing a condom and slipping it on with quick precision. Although I wasn't fully recovered, seeing his dick pointing at my slippery wet center sent an ocean of untamed lust racing through me.

"Can I fuck you now?"

"Yes, Sir." The words fell shakingly from my lips. I wanted to touch him but was unable to do *shit* but be at his mercy, a slave to the anticipation he had so quickly rebuilt in me. A deep sigh left me when the velvety head grazed my lower lips and stirred my wet heat around, teasing and making me flex against the restraints holding me in place.

He teased repeatedly, and I begged like I was being held at gunpoint. "Please, Sir. I need more. Please, I need it." I had to know what that dick felt like. It wasn't a want, but a desperate need that had me pulling against the restraints so hard, I was sure I was bruising my wrist and legs.

This was the part of the game that played your mind and had you willing to do anything for him to give you the goods you knew he was capable of dishing out. He kept teasing the hot head around my slick opening to the point that tears were pooling to the surface of my eyes. I wanted him to fuck me so badly, my pleas sounded like the calls of a trapped animal. I even had the wrinkled and tearstained, cry face to match my begging words.

He dragged the head over my lower lips, making them smack before letting the hot tip of the slick head slide across my swollen clit. My chest shot up from a hard gasp of surprise when he lifted and slapped his dick against my stomach and left it there.

The visual of how big he was lying against my stomach and how hot and heavy his dick felt caused me to swallow an even mix of lust and anxiety. My angst wasn't from fear. I'd reached a point where I didn't give a shit if it hurt or left damage. I needed to be fucked.

"I wanted you in this position because I want you to remember me, Mystery."

I'd remember him, all right, with every bow-legged limp I took for the rest of my days if he sent his dick as far as the visual display indicated it could go. He smiled like he knew what I was thinking; *That he was going to turn my belly button from an innie to an outie from the inside.* I was desperate enough to let him do it.

He drew back, placed the head at my opening, and began easing the tip in. The thick head parted my lips wide before he shoved in a few inches. The view and physical sensation had me gasping in delight while tears of joy slipped down my cheeks.

Sir didn't start with hard pounding. No, he teased his way in, making my ass cheeks flex, and my thigh muscles tighten in a useless attempt to get him in faster. "More, please, Sir," I begged shamelessly, my gaze so heavy with need, I could hardly lift my watery eyelids.

With every plunge in, I got wetter and hotter and more excited. He knew what he was doing, making me want more with every glide. My juices were leaking so fluidly that my pussy made slurping sounds for him. "More, Sir," I moaned, greedily. I could get off on what he was doing to me, but I was so aroused that I welcomed the pulsing stretch he delivered.

By the time he was fully seated inside me, I was literally sagging against the restraints from the strain of exertion I'd put on my muscles, and tears were streaking down my face. I believed his intention was to have my muscles too spent to tense up, and to leave me so emotionally wrecked that his deep penetration would be all the healing I needed.

He backed all the way out so that the head kissed my opening and plunged back in to the hilt, causing me to release every drop of oxygen from my lungs and suck it all back in when he repeated the soul-stirring thrust. I'd forgotten about being tied up, exposed, and at the mercy of someone trained in all manner of pleasure-torture.

He kept a tight grip on my thighs, near the area where my legs were held by the restraints. Repeatedly, he plunged into me with long and deep thrusts that hit so hard, the chains attached to the restraints holding my legs in place rattled and thumped while my back was being driven into the back of the leathered bench.

Since my legs were secured in the air, the swinging action gave him more momentum to pound the shit out of me with the force of gravity helping him. He pulled out his slippery smooth heat until the head crested again. His dick was so slick with my wetness that it glistened against the light like glass before he drove it back in deeply, to the root, balls to the wall, head slamming against the back.

My lungs had given up the fight, and I took in oxygen whenever I could. He hit a depth that left a tingling ache in my stomach while the head pummeled my cervix, making it vibrate. I screamed so hard, the mirror above reflected a vibrating image of us. Unable to close my legs and move my arms, the restrictions should have sparked fear, but it tipped the addicting high I was experiencing off the scales.

With each impacting blow, he was leaving a mark on me that would never be forgotten. My pussy clenched and sucked and gushed, and the sweet penetration drove me wild with the pleasure rush it gave off.

The sting of the overwhelming fullness was almost too much because it reached in and snatched at an orgasm. The sweet promise of relief was no longer held in suspense, and I expressed my enjoyment through a wild outburst of screams. "Sir. Oh, fuck! Yes!" I yelled out while the rest of my shuddering body parts were locked into place.

Just when the pleasure grew intense enough to boil my blood until it sizzled under my flesh, I started begging. "Sir, can I…oh! Can I..." I couldn't speak the words I desperately needed to say. "Come?" I screamed before I came so hard that the sensation rippled through me as his slow strokes continued to milk my orgasm.

He reached over me and gripped the frame above my shoulders for leverage, gave one last push, and stayed buried deep as his throbbing dick jumped inside me. The orgasmic afterglow merged with the erratic thump in my pussy, keeping me in the haze of my high.

The slight tug he gave to the nipple leash lit waves of sharp, raw pleasure that easily jumpstarted my orgasm as the quick surge zipped from my chest and raced down to my pulsing core.

"Sir, can I come again?" I yelled, knowing I was on the verge of exploding because his dick was still hard and throbbing inside me. "Yes," he growled through his own frenzied release, and I spasmed, experiencing for the first time, multiple orgasms.

He'd quoted me three orgasms, but whatever connection he'd hotwired between my leashed nipples, his dick, and my pussy had milked out three explosive orgasms and two mini ones for good measure.

Moments later, after I had come down from The Pleasure Mountains, he backed out of me. I was unable to stand when he released me from the restraints, so he walked me to and sat me on the bed while he drew me a bath.

He returned and carried me to the bathroom before lowering my sex-drenched body into the tub. When he asked to join me, there was no other answer in my brain except, "Yes, Sir."

He placed me between his legs and bathed me with strokes so tender I had to wonder if a different man had climbed into this tub with me. He said it was called after-care. The real shocker was that I didn't mind reciprocating the tender calm and easing warmth he lavished on me.

CHAPTER EIGHT

Camina

After he had dried and wrapped me in a soft fluffy towel, Sir walked me back into the Wicked Truth. I went for my clothes, thinking that this had been one of the best nights of my sexual life, but he stopped me with a firm hand on my forearm.

"You thought the bath meant that I was getting you prepared to go home?"

I nodded. "Yes, Sir." He shook his head while a sneaky grin spread over his sexy lips.

"That bath was all about getting your body relaxed and ready for another round."

My clueless gaze bumped into his devilish one.

"In the treatment room, I asked if I could bring you pleasure in other ways, and you told me only if I let you do the same to me. It's your turn, Mystery."

Where had this man been my whole life? He'd listened and remembered my words, but the smirk on his face held a devious edge I was learning to expect.

"I need to come again, but I want you to do it without touching me."

"Say what?" I squinted at him. "Sir," I quickly added, staring like he'd spoken alien. Every time I'd taken control sexually in my past, I'd been accused of being too aggressive, but Sir had fixed that problem because he wasn't giving me the option of touching him.

He took a seat on the side of the bed facing the city view, waiting while I stood there not knowing what the hell to do. I had one of the hottest men I'd laid eyes on, naked and waiting for me to make him come, and my brain had stalled.

I considered what he would have done from his kinky perspective, and he sat there patiently, letting me work things out in my head. What could he do that would make me come without his touch?

Once I'd formed a plan in my head, I shopped his toy-shrouded walls, picking out the ones I planned to use. He didn't hide the roaring excitement that had him sitting tall and staring with an eagerness I could literally feel.

After placing the toys on the seat cushion, I dragged a chair that resembled something from the medieval times, into position. I aligned it so that it stopped about six feet away from the bed and put my back to the view.

The buttery soft black leather bottom of the chair caressed my ass when I dropped my towel and took the seat. The chair's intimidating spiked arms and the thick, shiny chains that made up the back gave it a daring personality.

The flickers of fiery passion reflected in Sir's gaze were revving up my confidence. I loved everything about this scene, if not for anything other than to keep that hungry look on his face.

I laid back in the chair, letting the cold metal of the chains kiss the top of my back. The chains were pulled tight enough that an easy sway was the extent of my movement. The length and width of the chair allowed me to lift my feet and rest them atop the leathered seat bottom before letting my legs fall slowly apart.

Sir reacted with a hard swallow, his eyes dancing back and forth between my face and my pussy blooming open for him. His dick, the beautiful specimen it was, was as stiff and hard as the metal pressing into my back. The sight of the straining head, glistening with pre-cum from a distance, added fuel to my desire to keep this game going.

My fingers moved down my stomach until the middle one hovered above my clit, and my free hand gripped one of the thick metal spikes on the chair's arm to steady myself. The heat of the fire raging through me reached out and touched the sexy man in front of me, making him bite into his bottom lip as his chest rose and fell quicker with each breath he released.

"Sir," I called to him, my tone low and heavy with the heat of my blazing desires. "Yes, Mystery," he answered with an edgy tremble in his deep masculine tone.

"In this scene, your hand is my pussy, and my fingers will be your dick. Whatever I do with this dick—" I lifted my hand and licked up the length of my fingers, loving how he played along, sucking in a deep laboring breath like I was licking up his length.

He had gotten the point, but I finished. "You have to react to it with my pussy." He lifted his palm to his mouth and flicked his tongue against it in rapid strokes like he was licking my clit. The sight had me leaking and so damn hot, I inhaled and released a calming breath to keep my composure.

I sat my hand on my pussy, using my pointer and ring finger to spread my swollen lips apart. With my middle finger, I made delicate circles around my clit. The slippery movement of my bud under my finger poured fuel on my desire, and Sir was the flame. I choked on my moans, triggered by the rolling spikes of pleasure from my own touch. My nerve endings were lit with a pulsing need that flared higher with each stroke I made.

Sir matched my movements, using his fingertips to circle the leaking head of his dick. His length was so hard and heavy, he used his free hand to hold it in place. I lifted my knees higher, letting my legs fall open wider by pushing my back harder into the chained back of the chair and causing the metal to squeak out a groaning whine. A quick glance down showed that I was leaking enough to leave the black leather under me wet.

I slid my middle finger into my soaked hole, strumming the clenching muscles that licked at it. Sir matched my action, fisting his leaking tip. I worked my finger in and out with slow, teasing dips. The sight of him running his hand up and then down his shaft added to my trembling excitement.

"That's it, Mystery, you know how to turn me the fuck on," he whispered harshly. His lust-drenched facial expressions, heaving sighs, and the commanding way his hand slid up and down his thick dick was driving me to the blissful conclusion faster than I wanted to get there. My body rocked desperately against my hand, and I became so slick, one finger wasn't enough.

I eased my finger out, still watching him run his hand up his dick until it stopped at the tip. He didn't move again until I was inserting two fingers that I pumped into myself with a fierce need to smother the fire that was burning out of control.

"You like this game?" he asked between harsh breaths. "Yes, Sir," rushed out before a chest-shaking moan escaped. The sucking sounds my pussy was making were increasing in volume as I pumped my fingers faster, shoving them in deep and hard, and each downstroke sent my palm tapping against my hungry clit.

He fondled his balls and jerked his dick up and down with firm strokes that made the skin on his head stretch taut while precum seeped from the tip. I wasn't going to last much longer. The visual stimulation held major weight in this scene and had my body believing it was his dick tunneling through me versus my fingers.

The hard beat of my pulse thundered in my lower belly and sent jolts of fire racing straight to my pussy. My walls sucked and clenched along with my body's uncontrolled seizing, and my head felt light enough to float away from my shoulders.

Sir's hips flexed up with fast pumping movements, his hand working his dick so fast it was starting to blur.

His neck veins and the one in the center of his forehead popped up. He clenched his teeth hard but kept his eyes on me.

"I'm about to—"

"Me too—"

Neither of us finished our sentence. "Oh, shit," I screamed at the sudden explosion, my pussy pulsing so hard that the beat thumped in my ears and vibrated through my body. The toys I had gathered were being knocked to the floor. I continued to ram my fingers into myself, not knowing when I had inserted the third.

"Fuck!" Sir released a ragged roar, and the first shot of cum shot out and sprayed into the air like he'd released a pressure valve. More flowed from him, drizzling down his pumping fist, and another spurt shot out and landed on the flexing muscles of his thigh.

We were surrounded by every brand of sex toy, furniture, and equipment of anyone's kinky dream, but I had come undone by my hand and the sight of him. He made me realize that we didn't need anything but each other in the same room, and we had the ability to create magic together.

"Shit," I released, stretching out the word as my body fell into the orgasmic afterglow, an unprescribed drug with no harmful side effects. "That was intense," I admitted on a ragged breath.

"And fucking delicious," he said, his smile growing slowly across his handsome face. We sat there, breathing and smiling at each other until my temperature cooled.

"Can I have a taste?" he asked, letting his gaze that had grown hungry again drop to my soaked pussy. I couldn't accuse the man of not having any stamina; that was for damn sure. He was determined to make this a night I'd never forget. My pussy was as sore as fuck, but the strength of my desire outweighed my physical limitations and spoke truth into the words, mind-over-matter.

"Yes, Sir," I replied. "At this point, you can do whatever you want. Apparently, you've found a way to set my freak free from the prison I'd locked her in."

My comment made him release a chuckle while he stood and wiped himself clean with a wet towel. He made a slow approach in my direction, his heavy dick bobbing with each step before he stopped and stood before my limp and still spread open legs. I assumed he'd start fucking me since we were aligned, and his dick was iron-hard again. Instead, he leaned in until his lips met mine in a tender kiss.

He backed away and dropped to his knees, his face expressing an all-about-business promise, stamped with a seal of confidence to put my pussy out of commission for good.

He took his time cleaning the wetness away with a wet towel and checking to make sure I wasn't too sore to continue. He started our third or fourth round with a fiery kiss, connecting his lips with my lower ones before blowing at the wetness that had begun to coat me.

When he drew my clit between his lips, he released, sucked, and pulled at it again. The delicious tugging sent my eyes rolling to the back of my head. He didn't lift his head until he'd licked me clean. I hadn't been sexed in so long, I must have had a stored reserve of wetness because I continued to leak for him.

"I need to see you come again," he said like he had the power to make it happen at will. When he extracted the fingers he had plucking at my g-spot, I whined, "Please, Sir, don't stop." He ignored my plea, and a gripping silence fell and stilled us both, our gazes locked. Then—

Smack!

He had smacked my pussy, and I didn't know whether I should scream or moan because every nerve ending down there had gone haywire. My eyes met his, and I was sure he read the *what the fuck* mixed with the *I think I like it* swimming in my contemplative expression.

Smack!

Lord, calm my freak down because I liked this weird shit. The way my pussy flooded reinforced that the freak in me was also a slut. Was pussy smacking a thing?

Smack!

He didn't hold back this time, and my breath was caught up someplace in my throat and chest, and my begging eyes were on him while I silently chanted, "*Do it again.*"

To my disappointment, he didn't. Instead, he spread my legs wider, sending them across the arms of the chair. My calves resting between the thick spikes made it appear that my legs were sticking out of the mouth of a giant metal-toothed animal.

Smack!

He'd held back because the surprise of being pussy smacked was more stimulating than knowing it was coming. He wasted no time, lining his stiff dick up and slamming into me with no mercy.

"Motherfuck!" I shouted before reaching back and taking a hold of the chains at my back. He leaned in closer without interrupting his stroke and gripped the chair back, using it for leverage to pound into me harder and deeper.

He didn't stop until he'd beaten my pussy to death. We came together again, a scream and a roar loud enough to shake the window panes. At this point, I'd lost count of how many times he'd coaxed me into orgasm while lavishing me with the kind of punishment I didn't even know I needed.

CHAPTER NINE

Colson

I came awake with a rush of excitement coursing through me, and my gaze automatically fell on Mystery. She was the first woman in three years that had slept in my arms and the first that I hadn't invited to stay the night purely out of an obligation to give proper aftercare. The situation was plain and simple, I wanted Mystery, and I didn't even know her real name.

The daylight spilling in past my drapes was the last thing I wanted to see. It meant the perfect *Mystery* that had blown into my life was leaving me, and I'd never see her again. I knew my thinking was irrational, but I wasn't ready to let go. She would be the perfect sub, one that would make me work so fucking hard to break her that I'd break right along with her. She could take me being who I needed to be when it came to sex and my dominating nature while giving it back with as fierce a desire as mine.

Her questionnaire had informed that she tended to be rough around the edges when it came to intimacy and sex. Our rough edges could be released in whatever fashion our hearts' desired and laid smooth in the aftermath.

Later, the sight of her getting dressed and ready to walk away for good put a heavy ache in my chest.

"I'd like to see you again," I blurted, drawing her attention away from the sexy black heel in her hand. There was a hint of distress and a heavy dose of concern in the expression she cast in my direction.

"This was supposed to be a one-time thing. We finish the *date*. I submit a recommendation to 'The Market,' and that's it, no strings."

I stepped up so close that her quick breaths bounced off my chest before I leaned in to put my face in front of hers. "With you, I want the strings."

Her face crinkled. "You don't even know my name. I don't know yours. How can you say you want more when all we did was have sex? A one night stand." She dropped her gaze back to the shoe. "It was overwhelmingly good, snatch your soul sex, but still," she muttered under her breath, lifting the heel to her foot this time.

I slipped a finger under her chin to reclaim her attention, making sure my gaze bored into hers. "Don't lie to yourself. You know as well as I do that we are more than 'soul-snatching sex.'"

Her shoulders dropped, and she released a loud humph as the heel slipped from her hand and hit the floor. I bent and took a knee before her, picking up the shoe and taking her foot in my hand.

"Tell me your name?"

She didn't respond, but she watched me place each shoe back on her feet before placing a tight grip around her ankles, pinning her feet to the floor and keeping her in place. Her tongue passed over her lips at my suggestive action, and I tightened my grip until her nipples pebbled under her dress. The notion that I could turn her on with an aggressive hold around her ankles put an arrogant smirk on my face.

When I let go, she stood, and I remained on the floor, staring up at her.

"Camina. My name is Camina Harrison."

My eyes fell closed because her voice kissed every part of me. Her name was as beautiful as she was, and the syllables repeatedly played in my head. I stood and couldn't help reaching out to feather my fingers along her cheek. "Camina," I whispered, more to myself than her. "My name is Colson Richards," I said, introducing myself.

"Colson, I have to admit, I'm horrible at anything that may be considered a relationship."

I leaned in and nipped her ear, leaving my lips to hover there. "You hadn't met the right one yet, and *our* relationship will make that traditional shit look like a bag of trash."

"And you're him? The right one?" Her raised brows were more expressive than her question.

"Yes," I replied with no hesitation and more sure about us than I'd been about anything. "Give me your phone," I told her, holding my hand out expectantly. She reached into her purse, handed it over, and watched me store my number in it before calling my phone so that I'd have her number.

Even though confident I'd see her again, there was still a nagging ache in my stomach at the notion that she was leaving. She must have been experiencing a similar ache because she remained in place, standing in front of me and holding my gaze with reluctance peeking from hers.

"I'm not ready to let you go, Camina." My admission caused her small smile to break free.

"And I'm not ready to go, but I have to prepare for my family get-together tomorrow. I'll never hear the end of it if I don't."

"How about I go meat shopping with you" I volunteered, barely containing the grin that was itching to come out. We had come full circle in a way. This had started with her discussing meat shopping for her family function. She'd had no idea that I'd been hanging on to her every word and sneaking distorted peeks at her that were reflected back at me in the glass portion of the booth.

"You'd do that. You'd go meat shopping with me?"

"Yes. You made an excellent choice choosing me, but I wouldn't want you picking out the wrong type of meat."

We laughed together. It was a genuine action that tickled my spirit and gave me a spark of joy I hadn't felt in a long while.

CHAPTER TEN

Colson

Even though I tried, I couldn't let go. Yesterday, I'd gone with Camina to her place so she could shower and change into comfortable meat-shopping clothes. I had assisted her in picking out all of the meats that she was supplying for her family gathering. No less than an hour later, I had returned to her house, offering to help her marinate and refrigerate the meats.

When night began to fall, I didn't ask for permission but kicked off my shoes and made myself at home. Her not protesting my possessive behavior had landed us in her shower, followed by me taking a tour of her house to show her how her furniture, clothes, and other household ornaments could be used as props in our sexual escapades.

Another day was greeting us now, and I still hadn't had enough of her. She came awake with a start, feeling the weight of my presence at her side and in her bed. She peeled her eyes open and stared through a sleepy squint.

"Good morning, my beautiful Mystery. I made you breakfast," I announced, hoping she didn't think I was being creepy for making myself so at home in her house. She tucked the sheets around her chest while sitting up, despite me having intimate details of every inch of her. I strolled around, comfortable in my nakedness, wanting her to get to know every inch of me.

"Good morning," she finally responded. The black-out drapes were still drawn, and the bedside clock had been kicked off of the nightstand and had landed someplace out of view.

"Let me grab your breakfast," I stated, walking away and unwilling to allow that frown that dented her forehead to seep into her brain and turn into second thoughts about us.

Her face lit with a vibrant glow and a warm smile at the sight of me returning with a serving tray filled with life-giving coffee, perfectly-browned toast, scrambled eggs, crispy bacon, and orange juice. I set the tray across her legs and perched on the edge of the bed next to her. That questionnaire had given me a snapshot of her likes and dislikes, without all of the drawn-out explanations that popped up in conversations or omissions that kept you in the dark.

She must have used the bathroom while I was in the kitchen because her hair, that I had tested the strength of last night, was pulled back into a neat ponytail. I also wanted to see if she would have any trouble swallowing. Not only had I taught her the first stages of conquering her gag reflex, but I had made her beg me to keep shoving my dick down her throat.

"Wow! This looks wonderful," she stated around a piece of bacon that had made its way between her sexy lips. "Mmm. It's good," she mouthed. She took a hearty sip of coffee, and I picked up the half strip of bacon she hadn't finished and ate it.

"You're serious about us nontraditionally dating?"

"Deadly serious," I replied before sipping from her coffee cup and loving the way her gaze traced my lips.

"We were each other's booty call," she stated. The apprehension in her tone made her voice crack.

A sarcastic grin I knew was laced with the arrogance I felt sat perched on my lips. "We are more to each other than you understand right now. We have so much more to experience together. You get me. When I take out rope, a blindfold, or cuffs, you don't shy away from it. I love that you have no problem letting me figure out what you might like. I enjoyed going meat shopping with you yesterday. I like your confidence and that you don't apologize for who you are in public and especially not with me. Do you have any idea how long it's been since I've casually hung out with a woman? How long it's been since I've slept at a woman's house?"

She fought the little twitch forming on her lips at my revealing words while her eyes followed the fork full of fluffy eggs I lifted to her mouth. I groaned at the sight of the fork sliding between her lips, and a smile broke free while she chewed and watched me.

"Besides," I said, shifting to adjust my stiffening dick that was inching up my thigh since I was still as naked as the day I was born. "I can't bear the thought of another man getting what feels like mine, what tastes like mine, and what smells like mine." I leaned in so closely that she stopped moving. "What *is* all mine." I dragged the words out, loving the lust that filled her gaze. "That pussy even sounds like mine when she's singing love songs to my dick. I can't wait until that soreness heals so she can take the beating I have planned for her."

Her nipples had tightened, and the lust hanging heavily in her gaze was a welcomed sight.

"When you put it that way," she said, finally continuing to chew and speaking with a hand in front of her mouth. "You make it impossible to say no."

She bit into her toast and fed me from the same piece, watching with keen interest as it disappeared into my mouth. Once she was done eating, she shifted against the pillows and gawked at my stiff, bobbing dick while I carried the dishes back to her kitchen.

***

Camina

A thunderous crash followed by the rumble of loud voices had me hopping out of my bed like it had caught fire. I grabbed the nine-millimeter I kept hidden in the secret compartment in my headboard and threw on my robe before dashing through my bedroom door.

Making it into my living room, I froze, stopped dead in my tracks at the scene that had unfolded in my house. Colson was standing in the middle of my living room with the dishes at his feet because he was using his hands to cover his dick. With its size, his hands didn't really hide *everything,* given that he'd left my bedroom naked with a raging hard-on.

He'd unknowingly marched into the living room and had made it as far as the wide-open space near the couch. My mother was standing there with her mouth hanging open, along with my Uncle Ralph and Aunt Lou-ann, my cousin Kenzie, and my brother Caleb.

They all stood there, frozen statues in my dining-kitchen area that opened to my living room. They were in such a state of awe that they hadn't acknowledged me enough to even notice me shoving my pistol in the pocket of my thick robe.

None of them had the decency to turn around and stop staring while Colson stood there, flashing them his prize-winning smile. My table had platters of food sitting atop it, so they must have arrived early for the get-together.

"Oh, my, my, my. I haven't seen anything that big since... phew, child." My mother stated this under her breath, but under her breath meant low-key audible enough for all to hear.

"Claudette, you done said a mouthful. Umh. Umh. Umh. That sure is something," my aunt added to my mother's comment before she turned to my uncle, who attempted to cover her eyes with his hands.

"He almost got you beat, honey," Aunt Lou-ann whispered loudly to my Uncle Ralph, patting him absently on the hand she kept dodging from blocking her view.

I did my best to pretend I hadn't heard the commentary and fought not to pass out with embarrassment. My brain must have stopped communicating with my body because my thoughts never reached a conclusion. There was so much wrong happening in this situation that right had left the building. Colson naked in my living room. My family gawking shamelessly at him. Them wondering who the hell he was, since as far as they knew, I was single. Me running out of my bedroom, half robed.

My cousin Kenzie was standing there with a shit-eating grin across her face, smacking her chewing gum and sending her eyes volleying between Colson and me. My brother had his signature right eye raised high on his forehead, and his grin rivaled my cousin's.

"What are ya'll doing here so early?" I asked, pushing through the thick curtain of shock and embarrassment that had gripped me, and stepping in front of Colson.

"That man must have put that thang on you to make you forget the time. It's a quarter to one," Kenzie was way too happy to inform. "We are here at our usual time to help set up."

"But, we can *see* you have other plans," my brother chimed, not allowing a break in the commentary. He tapped a stiff finger against his watch teasingly.

"Um hum," came a few murmurs of agreement from the Peanut Gallery, and my brother dotted the air with a dramatic finger where Colson's dick would be, if I wasn't in the way, to drive home his point. I glanced back and noticed Colson was back there, smiling and not the least bit embarrassed.

"Please accept my apology, everyone. It's my fault that Mystery..." He cleared his throat. "I mean, Camina, lost track of time," he said, driving home what my family's one-track minds were already wrapped securely around. He wasn't any better than my family and appeared almost eager to egg them on.

"You have nothing to apologize for, baby," my mother told Colson. "Believe me, I'm glad you're here." She grinned with pride gleaming in her eyes. She didn't care if it was the clown from the movie, *It*, as long as *it* was a man.

My mother had been *literally* praying for me to find a man. She'd been praying to the church about it on Sundays. The looks I received when I went to church some Sunday's were bad enough, but having members of the congregation running up to me in public and giving me hugs and pitying looks gave life to my loser status.

However, I'd never dreamed my family would walk into what they were never supposed to see with Colson and me. I reminded myself that things could have been worse. At least they hadn't walked in on me calling him *Sir,* begging him for his kinky loving, or him using his expert-level rope and bondage skills on me.

"I bet you forgot all about the cookout. I can't blame you, but did you at least remember to pick up the meat?" Kenzie asked, and I didn't miss her eyes landing on Colson and dropping low.

"Yes. I remembered," I replied and cast a quick glance at my mother and Aunt Lou-ann, who had no interest in me because their roving eyes were mapping a way around me to Colson. My brother had side-stepped his nosey ass to the left about a good four feet to adjust his view.

"You can put your damn four eyes back in your head now, Lou-ann. You've gotten all the free looks you're going to get. That boy might look white, but he got black in him where it counts," Uncle Ralph imparted his twisted wisdom and made the heat of my embarrassment flare higher.

I prayed the ridiculous comment hadn't insulted Colson, but hearing him chuckle behind me said he didn't mind being the star of this scene. The man had a dungeon called, *Wicked Truth* in his house, so this incident wasn't as big a deal for him as it was for me.

My face was so hot that it was a degree away from combusting. Colson and I were far enough in the open that the walk-of-shame back to the bedroom would give everyone a full view of his ass.

"Excuse me, but will you all have some decency and turn around instead of gawking and being nosey so he can at least walk back to the bedroom?" I asked, hoping they would do me this one small favor.

"Nosey is what we do best," Kenzie replied. "Who is this nice tall drink of water that met us with his dick?"

"Nice, big, and thick one too," my brother muttered.

"Watch your mouth lil girl, and that goes for you too, lil stanky-tail boy. Y'all ain't old enough to be using them grown words," Uncle Ralph reprimanded, glaring above the rim of his glasses at Kenzie and Caleb. Kenzie cut her eyes at him and ran a hand over her pregnant belly to emphasize that she *was* grown enough.

All except Uncle Ralph continued to peek around me to take in more of Colson.

"This is my friend, Colson. Colson, my rude family," I said with a weak hand gesture to make one of the most awkward introductions I'd ever made in my life.

"Hi, everyone. I'm sorry I couldn't have met you in a more dignified way," Colson greeted.

"You look pretty dick-tified to me. All up in my niece's house running around in your dick-day suit like you're paying mortgage here," Uncle Ralph replied, chuckling at his own silliness while the rest of the group joined in, um humming and agreeing with the ridiculous comment.

Mortified didn't begin to cover my reality as a few more teasing, "Hello's" and "Nice to meet you's," followed my uncle's comments. My eyes closed on a silent prayer, begging for this to be a dream.

"Now that the introductions are done. Where is the damn meat? The kind we can cook, please," my brother blurted with a teasing smirk.

"Excuse us," I said before gripping Colson's arm and dragging him away since my family wasn't going to give up the opportunity to be nosey and rude. Colson bowed slightly in their direction before turning and walking away like he wasn't butt-ass naked. I lifted the long tail of my robe in an attempt to cover his ass.

"Ooh wee, and he got a nice tight ass too," Caleb commented, and I glanced back in time to see him and Kenzie bumping arms. "Jesus. I need me a church fan," someone said, keeping the shameless teasing going.

Once we were back in the bedroom, Colson hopped into his clothes. "I'm sorry, Colson. I didn't know it was so late, or I would have warned you about my family's habit of letting themselves into my house."

"It's okay. You told me about the cookout, but I thought it would be later this evening."

"It is, but Uncle Ralph is the barbeque expert, so he'll work the pit while we set up the tables and display the food that the rest of the family is bringing. You can stay if you want to," I told him. "Honestly, they're going to demand you stay now that they have seen you and are no doubt out there creating a list of questions they have for us. Since they found you naked, they are going to get *very* personal."

He stepped closer with a wide grin that put an automatic smile on my face.

"After meeting your family the way that I just did, I'd say that we are further along in our relationship than some married couples. When I told you I had more to give, I meant it. I love you being my Mystery, and there is so much more about you that I need to solve."

His eyes flashed with dark hunger before he dialed it down. "Besides, there is no way I'm leaving you here alone to face what I know is coming."

If my smile had grown any wider, my cheeks would have brushed my lashes. He had just given me a big chunk of the *something more* that I hadn't expected this soon in our *relationship*. It was funny that one of the biggest surprises in my life held the key to satisfying me sexually and had a leg-up on fulfilling me emotionally.

Colson had been introduced to both my family and me, meat first. However, I believed anyone who could get through an introduction like the one he'd just breezed through could get through anything.

I went up on my toes and flung my arms around his neck, more sure now than ever about us. All I could think as he squeezed me tight in his grip was that a trip to go *meat* shopping may just turn out to be the best thing to ever happen to me!

***End of Mystery Meat ***

**Please stay tuned for an excerpt
from Author L. Loren.**

AUTHOR L. LOREN – EXCERPT

Coming November 25, 2020

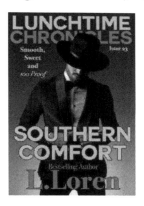

Southern Comfort Blurb

Garrison Daniels is on the run. After his failed attempt to murder his brother and overthrow his father as boss of The Enterprise Faction, his days are numbered. So why is he in a mansion filled to the brim with his father's deadliest associates? One word… Malina.

Malina Gardner is getting married. Her estranged lover could never resist disrupting her marriage ceremony and that's just what she is counting on. As the Enterprise's top assassin this is the only way to get her mark out in the open. But Malina isn't ready for what happens when they finally see each other again.

She has always been his ride or die, but what happens when the sentiment becomes reality?

Southern Comfort is an interracial erotic romance (BWWM) with a HEA. It is a part of the Lunchtime Chronicles series which can be read as standalone novels.

WARNING: This book contains explicit sex, violence and graphic language.

PROLOGUE

"Garrison, I love you more than life, but I can't marry you."

"Why the hell not, Malina?"

"You know, as well as I do, why not."

I laid there watching the woman I have loved since we were in middle school playing touch football in the gym together. She was leaving my bed once again to get back home before her father found out she was gone. She slid her sexy black lace thong up those silky-smooth thighs and covered the best pussy in all the world. I loved watching her get undressed, but she was just as sensual putting her clothes back on. How does that work?

"You already know why, but if I need to spell it out for the millionth time then I will. My father will not allow me to marry anyone who is not the boss. The only exception is for me to marry the one who is next in line. Since you are neither, I can't marry you."

Her words caused me to rub my hand down my face in frustration. She was right. I knew the rules. It wasn't just her father who mandated this rule. It was written in the bylaws. Jesus himself may as well have come down from heaven and said it to be so. Nobody in The Enterprise would ever go against the bylaws. It was the only way to keep order within the organization. The punishment for violating the bylaws was death. No exceptions.

"Yeah, but I am in the bloodline. I may not be the firstborn, but I am the son of the boss. That should count for something."

"I agree, baby but we don't make the rules. The only way my name will be Malina Garrison is if I were to either marry your father or your runaway, cowardice brother."

I shot up out of the bed fueled by anger. Grabbing Malina by her throat, I growled in her face.

"Any man who even thinks about marrying you will meet his end by my hands. Don't fucking test me, Lina. You know how jealous I can be. I don't care if they are my family."

She smiled up at me, but her eyes held that sexy edge that all assassins had. She could end me right here in my bedroom if she wanted, but she loved me. I knew she would never harm one hair on my head.

"That shit is so hot, G. However, if you're not planning on sticking that big cock of yours in me immediately, I suggest you stop choking me. Otherwise, I may see it as a threat and end both of our lives right here."

She wasn't playing either. I could feel her Mark IV pressing into my side. It was her signature weapon of choice, and my lady wasn't shy about using it. In fact, she was the best I had ever seen with any kind of weapon. She knew if she killed me, there would be a hefty price on her head. Before I could respond, she leaned forward and licked my face. God, I loved her.

"Stay the night with me, Malina. I hate not waking up to you every day. I need to see your grumpy morning face."

"And just what will you do to make me smile?"

"Stay with me and I'll show you."

"I want to, but I can't. I am going to my engagement party tomorrow afternoon. My father will be looking for me. I need to get home before he notices I slipped out."

My hand dropped to my side and I took a step back. I had to be hearing things. *Who the fuck was she supposed to marry if it wasn't me?*

"Engagement?" What the hell, Malina? When did this happen? And to who?"

For the first time since I met her many years ago, I saw tears in Malina's eyes. The sadness there was unbearable. If my own heart wasn't breaking, I would have tried to help her. I needed her to answer my questions. I already knew the answer, but I needed to hear her say it.

"My father announced it to me last night at dinner. I have been promised in an arranged marriage. If I do not agree, I will be disowned and disavowed from The Enterprise. No longer under their protection. Once that happens, my life will mean nothing. I will be easy pickings for anyone who wants to kill me. I have a lot of enemies. He didn't come right out and say it, but I am smart enough to put two and two together. If I want to live, I must marry the man my father has chosen."

My lungs deflated from the news she just delivered. The room started spinning as I tried to understand what she was saying. No way could I allow my love to marry another man. My head would explode if she simply smiled in greeting at another.

"And who is that? Give me the name of the man I have to knock off."

"Donavan Daniels."

"FUCK!" Now, I'm going to have to kill my own father.

End of Southern Comfort Excerpt

Acknowledgement

I'd like to say an extra special thank you to Author Siera London for extending a warm invite into the Lunchtime Chronicle's world. I humbly appreciate her and the writing platform she has built and hope that it continue to spread joy to readers and inspiration to writers.

Thank you to my beta readers, Zanthia Shaw-Matthews and Lashonda Royal, who dedicated their time to reading this novella and providing excellent feedback. Zan, I'd like to say an extra special thank you for letting me know when something didn't make sense or when you realized it didn't sound up to my standard of writing. Your input made me dig deeper to add more depth and character to the manuscript, and I cannot say thank you enough for your time and invaluable advice.

Author's Note

Readers, my sincere thank you for taking a chance on me and for choosing to read my novella. Please leave a review letting me and others know what you thought of the book. If you enjoyed it or any of my other books, please pass them along to friends or anyone you think would enjoy them.

Other Titles by Keta Kendric

The Twisted Minds Series:

Twisted Minds #1
Twisted Hearts #2
Twisted Secrets #3
Twisted Obsession #4
Twisted Revelation #5
Twisted **D**eception – Coming 2021

The Chaos Series:

Beautiful Chaos #1
Quiet Chaos #2
Hidden Chaos – Coming 2021

Stand Alone:

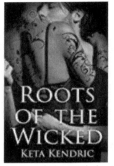

Roots of the Wicked

MC Novella:

Carolina Reaper

Connect on Social Media

Subscribe to my Newsletter for exclusive updates on new re-
leases, sneak peeks, deleted scenes, and much more. Join my
Facebook Readers' Group, where you can live-chat about my
books, enjoy contests, raffles, and giveaways.

Twitter: https://twitter.com/AuthorKetaK

Instagram: https://instagram.com/ketakendric

Pinterest: https://www.pinterest.com/authorslist/

Bookbub: https://www.bookbub.com/authors/keta-kendric

Newsletter: https://mailchi.mp/c5ed185fd868/httpsmailchimp

Facebook Page: https://www.facebook.com/AuthorKetaK-
endric

Goodreads:https://www.goodreads.com/user/show/73387641-
keta-kendric

Facebook Readers' Group: https://www.face-
book.com/groups/380642765697205/

Made in the USA
Middletown, DE
29 August 2024

59656232R00073